BLOOD ON THE MONEY 3

J-Blunt

Lock Down Publications and
Ca$h Presents
Blood on the Money 3
A Novel by **J-Blunt**

J-Blunt

Lock Down Publications
P.O. Box 944
Stockbridge, Ga 30281

Visit our website
www.lockdownpublications.com

Copyright 2021 by J-Blunt
Blood on the Money 3

Lock Down Publications
Like our page on Facebook: Lock Down Publications @
www.facebook.com/lockdownpublications.ldp
Book interior design by: **Shawn Walker**
Edited by: **Jill Alicea**

Stay Connected with Us!

Text **LOCKDOWN** to 22828 to stay up-to-date with new releases, sneak peeks, contests and more…

Submission Guideline.

Submit the first three chapters of your completed manuscript to ldpsubmissions@gmail.com, subject line: Your book's title. The manuscript must be in a .doc file and sent as an attachment. The document should be in Times New Roman, double-spaced and in size 12 font. Also, provide your synopsis and full contact information. If sending multiple submissions, they must each be in a separate email.

Have a story but no way to send it electronically? You can still submit to LDP/Ca$h Presents. Send in the first three chapters, written or typed, of your completed manuscript to:

LDP: Submissions Dept
P.O. Box 944
Stockbridge, Ga 30281

DO NOT send original manuscript. Must be a duplicate.

Provide your synopsis and a cover letter containing your full contact information.

Thanks for considering LDP and Ca$h Presents.

Acknowledgements

I have to begin by giving a big shout out to my amazingly beautiful and smart niece, Honesty Thomas. You are a blessing, baby girl. Maria Sanchez, thank you for blessing me with your love and support. Beauty, the good times outweigh the bad. Nothing worth having is easily gained.

A special thank you to the fans and supporters of J-Blunt. Every time I write, I always try my best to make the next book better than the last one. Thanks for the feedback and the reviews. I love all of y'all and it ain't nothing you can do about it!

Connect with me on Facebook @ Author J-Blunt

J-Blunt

BOOK I: KEEP YOUR EYES ON YOUR ENEMIES

ENEMY - A PERSON WHO HATES ANOTHER AND WISHES OR TRIES TO INJURE HIM.

SOMETIMES THE ENEMY CAN'T BE EASILY IDENTIFIED.

THE WORST KIND OF ENEMY IS THE ONE YOU DON'T SEE COMING.

WHILE IT IS IMPORTANT TO KNOW WHY THE ENEMY IS AN ENEMY, THE MORE IMPORTANT QUESTION TO ASK YOURSELF IS, DO YOU KNOW WHO YOUR ENEMIES ARE?

FOR MOST PEOPLE, YOUR WORST ENEMY IS YOU.

WE PICK OURSELVES APART. BEAT OURSELVES UP. CRITICIZE EVERYTHING WE DO.

OTHERS THINK TOO HIGHLY OF THEMSELVES. LIE TO THEMSELVES AND GET IN THEIR OWN WAY.

SO AFTER YOU SPEND SOME TIME DISCOVERING WHO YOUR WORST ENEMY IS, DECIDE HOW TO BEST DEFEND YOURSELF AGAINST HIM SO THAT YOU WON'T BE DEFEATED.

IF YOUR OWN WORST ENEMY IS YOU, SEARCH YOUR DEPTHS TO FIGURE OUT YOUR ISSUES AND DEAL WITH THEM ACCORDINGLY.

FAILING TO ADDRESS YOUR OWN ISSUES CAN BRING MORE DESTRUCTION UPON YOU THAN ALL YOUR ENEMIES COMBINED!

J-Blunt

CHAPTER 1

Being a boss is hard work! Especially when you are in the middle of a war. Not a real war with guns, rockets, and bombs. It was a cold war, like the United States and Soviet Union had back in the 80s. Threats had been made. Now I had to put myself in a position to win, and winning was a must. Failure was not an option. Bosses didn't fail!

"Oh, Carl! Yeah, daddy! Oh yeah!" Sissandra moaned, loving the way I was digging in them guts.

Sissandra was my twenty-year-old play toy. I met her two weeks ago while she was on her way to school at Northwestern University. When I seen the way her ass poked out in them jeans, I whipped the Bentley to the curb and took a shot. She was short, strapped, and fine enough to be my Woman Crush Wednesday for 52 weeks in a row. Pretty brown skin, long purple dreadlocks, big brown eyes, and titties big enough to feed all the starving kids in Africa. And that ass... Dayum, that ass!

"I want it all, big daddy! Gimme all that dick. Give it to me!" Sissandra called, squeezing my hands tightly.

She was on her knees, head in the sky, and I was behind her, holding both of her hands behind her back while I fucked her doggy style. Her thick ass couldn't take too much dick so I took it easy, giving her most, but not all of my shit. But now she wanted it all, and the pussy was so good that I couldn't wait to give it to her. So when she asked, I lifted one of my legs, thrusting my hips forward, smashing my pelvis into her big-ass booty. Our sweaty flesh smacked loudly as her ass cheeks rippled like a tidal wave.

"Oh God! Oh God! Oh God!" she cried.

"That's it, baby girl! You taking it all," I groaned, biting my bottom lip while trying to hold back my nut. Hearing her moans, watching that ass bounce, and being deep in her tight-ass pussy had me ready to bust.

"Damn, y'all couldn't wait for me to finish getting ready?" Simone asked.

I looked towards the door as Sissandra's cousin walked in the bedroom butt-ass naked. She had dark brown skin, a tall athletic body, little titties, and a small ass. But those lips! They were big and soft as cotton candy. And she knew how to suck dick.

"Early bird gets the worm," I managed, gritting my teeth and trying to hold off my nut a little longer.

"Okay, daddy! I can't take no more. Take it out!" Sissandra cried.

I couldn't stop. Not right now. Shit was feeling too good!

"Take that dick, cuz." Simone smiled, climbing on the bed and slapping Sissandra's big-ass booty. Lust shone in her eyes and I could see how bad she wanted to suck my dick.

"It's in my stomach, Carl! Oh shit! I can't take no more!" Sissandra cried.

"You ready for this?" I asked Simone, ready to explode.

She responded by lying on her side, face a few inches away from my hips drilling into Sissandra's ass. She even stuck out her tongue and started licking the side of her cousin's big bouncing ass. That did it for me. I let go of Sissandra's hands and snatched my dick from her pussy. Simone's mouth was waiting.

"Oh shit! Goddamn, girl!" I moaned.

Simone's big-ass lips wrapped around my dick and didn't let go. She sucked me hard while her hand pumped the base. It felt like I was skeeting out a gallon.

"Damn, girl! Ah, shit!" I groaned before falling onto the bed.

Simone kept on sucking even after my dick went soft and brought a nigga back to life like she had defibrillators in her mouth.

"Get that ass ready for me," I told Sissandra.

She was laying off to the side recovering while watching Simone suck my dick. At my command, Simone got on her knees and Sissandra got behind her. I watched her spread her cousin's cheeks apart and start licking. Simone let out a moan that vibrated through my dick and tickled my nuts. Sissandra stuck her tongue in Simone's ass and started using it like a small dildo. Then she moved her mouth and slipped in a finger. Simone stopped sucking my dick to let out another moan. Sissandra continued working her fingers in

Simone's ass, eventually slipping in two digits. Shit was nasty and sexy at the same time.

"Oh, yes! Ssss!" Simone moaned.

"Is it ready for me? " I asked, ready to get deep in that tight ass. Simone didn't want to give me the pussy. Only let me fuck one time. Said giving me the pussy made it feel like she was cheating on her man, who was doing time in Cook County jail. But I could fuck her in the ass and let her suck my dick all she wanted.

"She ready, daddy." Sissandra grinned.

I flipped Simone on her back and pushed her knees to her shoulders. Sissandra straddled her cousin reverse cowgirl, holding her feet while I aimed my dick.

"Get it wet."

Sissandra bent forward and dropped a loogie right on the tip of my dick as I pushed the head into Simone's ass.

"Sss! Ah!" Simone moaned.

I pushed more in and paused, letting her walls adjust. A few moments later, I gave her some more.

"Mmm, Carl! Yeah, baby."

"Gimme some more spit."

Sissandra spit on my dick as I pushed more in. When I was halfway in, I began to rock back and forth.

"Damn, Carl. That shit feel so good, nigga!" Simone moaned.

Sissandra watched with excitement in her eyes as I slipped more dick into her cousin's ass.

"Don't just watch. Get you some of that pussy," I encouraged.

Sissandra lowered her head and started eating Simone's pussy while I fucked her in the ass.

"Oh shit! Oh my God! Oh my God!" Simone screamed.

"Let her taste you, too," I told Sissandra.

She lowered herself onto Simone's face and they 69'd while I got deep in her ass. Both of my young freaks moaned in pleasure and I was loving life. A few minutes later, Simone came loudly, her anal walls clenching around my dick. Shit felt so good that I was ready to bust.

"Dayum, girl!" I roared, snatching my dick from Simone's ass.

Sissandra's lips were waiting. She didn't give head as good as Simone, but she drained every drop of nut from my balls.

"Damn, y'all young asses gon' kill me," I breathed, falling onto the bed.

"Where are your pills, baby?" Sissandra asked, fondling my rapidly shrinking dick. She wanted more.

"I don't know. I think they in the bathroom. One of y'all grab me a blunt," I mumbled, wiping sweat from my brow and checking the time on my phone. It was 9:34 p.m. I wasn't going to Triple Time until 11:00. The girls wanted to fuck until I left.

"I'ma go find the pills," Sissandra said, climbing from the bed. I watched her big beautiful ass bounce and clap as she walked to the master bathroom.

"You don't need no pills, baby," Simone said, handing me a blunt as she climbed back in bed. "All you need is my lips."

I lit the blunt and closed my eyes while Simone tried to bring me back to life. And that's when my phone rang. I opened my eyes to peek at the screen. It was Sergeant Snipes.

"What's good, Sarge?" I answered.

"You know the only time I call this late is if I got news."

My dick twitched in Simone's mouth.

"I'm listening."

"I found that faggot-ass politician."

A picture of Alderman Bishop Gains popped into my head. The thought of revenge got my dick hard.

"Where you at?"

"Old stomping grounds on the boat dock. We ready."

After hanging up the phone, I lay in bed for a moment, thinking about the cold war I was in. The tides had changed in my favor and I was about to strike a mighty blow.

"I found the pills," Sissandra sang, dancing into the room.

"We don't need them," Simone smiled, lifting her head to show off my prize.

"I'ma have to take a rain check, ladies," I said, sliding to the edge of the bed. "Something important came up and I gotta take care of it."

"Aw, man!" they whined.

"Y'all can stay here until I get back, or have Brandon drop y'all off at home. It's up to y'all," I told them as I got dressed.

The cousins shared a look.

"We staying," Simone said.

"Good. Be back in a little while."

After I got dressed, I walked into the living room, where three of my Triple Beam Team niggas lounged around. I took Brandon, Tito, and Webbie everywhere I went.

"Webbie and Tito, y'all rolling with me. Brandon, chill here and keep an eye on my company for me," I said, heading for the door.

The sweet taste of revenge danced across my taste buds during the drive to the old boating house on Lake Michigan. It was night, so the area was vacated - a perfect place to settle a score or get even. I damn near jumped from the backseat of the Bentley when we got to the spot. Excitement rushed through my body when I walked into the boat house. Sergeant Snipes sat lazily in a chair smoking a cigarette. His partner, Cooper, watched the windows. Alderman Gaines sat cuffed to a chair in the middle of the room.

"Ain't this a son of a bitch?" I smiled, eyeing the politician like he was an Audemers Peugeot watch.

"You're making a mistake, Carl. Let me out of this chair right now!" he demanded.

"I don't make mistakes, nigga. I make promises. And I promised that I was gon' get yo' bitch ass."

He looked me square in the eyes and laughed. "Let me tell you something, Carl. The people I work for make your bitch-ass Triple Beam Team look like Boys Scouts. I'm in the big leagues. I tried to give you a seat at the table, but you don't seem to value your life or that of your team. This is your last chance, Carl. Take these mutherfucking cuffs off me or I swear to God, on everything that I love, your whole family and your whole team will be in body bags by the end of the week!"

After he finished ranting, we had a staring contest. He didn't blink once.

"Let me tell you something, Alderman," I began, pulling a black .44 Bulldog from my waist and pointing it in his face. "I don't give a fuck about who you is or who you work for. This a TBT world, bitch!"

"Wait, Carl! Wait, goddamn it!" he yelled.

"What, nigga?"

"I work for Denzel Valentine. He sent me to talk to you."

I looked at Snipes. "Fuck is he talking about?"

The cop whistled. "That's Black Mafia shit right there. Black Billionaires Cartel."

I had heard of them in whispers, but nobody knew if the Black Billionaires Cartel actually existed. "That's some real shit?"

Snipes shrugged. "I probably heard the same shit as you. Don't nobody got proof they exist."

"We are real," Bishop Gaines spoke. "Behind the scene, we run the city. You don't want us as enemies. It's a BBC world."

I looked the politician in the eyes, weighing his words. He seemed sure about him and his niggas. But I didn't believe in Bigfoot, ghosts, or the Loch Ness monster.

"That's where you wrong, Bishop. It's a TBT world, and you just got voted out."

Boom!

The hand cannon kicked as fire spit from the barrel. The alderman's head jerked back when the bullet smacked into his forehead, blowing a hole in the back of his skull. The chair tipped and his lifeless body crashed to the ground. I stood over him for a moment and watched the life drain from his eyes.

"I owe you big for this one," I said, looking to my cop on pay.

"Make it up to me in zeros." He grinned.

"You know I will. You will take care of the body for me?"

"Don't I always? Feds will be all over this once they find out he's missing. Gotta make sure they don't ever find his body."

"Alright. Stop by the club when y'all finished and I'll have that bonus. Have a good night. "

After leaving the boathouse, I went to my club and partied like it was New Year's Eve. That's how much killing Bishop meant to me. Felt how JAY-Z must've felt when he tricked Damon Dash into selling his share of the record label, when all the while he was buying it for himself. I won!

When the club closed, I went back to my condominium with five bad bitches, and along with Sissandra and Simone, we had an orgy unlike any other. I took a Viagra and fucked until I passed out.

***

Boom, boom, boom, boom!

"Carl? Carl!"

I opened my eyes and tried to remember where the fuck I was. Made out my bedroom. Naked females sprawled across my bed. And somebody knocking on the door.

Boom, boom, boom!

"Carl, wake up, nigga! Carl!"

"Somebody at the door," a fine Asian woman said.

"Thanks, Captain Obvious," I mumbled while climbing out of bed. "Hold on. Here I come!" I called, stumbling to the closet to grab a robe. After covering my nakedness, I went to the door. "What, nigga?"

Brandon looked spooked. "Alderman Charles Brown is at the door!"

That got my attention. "Charles Brown is at my door right now?"

"Yeah. And he got some niggas with him. What you wanna do?"

I seen the desire to shoot it out in Brandon's eyes and let the image play in my head. Another politician dead. A multimillion dollar condominium shot up. Dead bodies everywhere. My face on the news.

"Who all here?" I asked, walking towards the living room.

"Tito and Webbie."

I walked into the living room and seen Tito and Webbie in defensive positions, guns pointed at the door.

"Somebody give me something. How the fuck this nigga find where I live?" I asked, heading for the door.

"I don't know," Brandon said, handing me a .45.

I checked the peephole and seen Charles Brown standing outside my door with four niggas that looked trained to go. "Who is it?"

"It's Charles Brown. Where is Carl? Tell him to open the door!"

I snatched the door open, catching them by surprise. "What you doing by my house, old man?"

He looked down at the gun in my hand and then in my eyes. "Put that shit away, boy. We ain't no goddamn street thugs," he lectured.

"This my house. Fuck you want?"

He gave an impatient look. "Let me in. We need to talk. "

Before I could agree or disagree, the old man walked into my house. His goons followed. When they seen my niggas holding heat, hostilities were exchanged without anyone saying a word.

"What do you want, old man?" I asked, closing the door, but keeping my pistol in plain sight.

"What happened to Alderman Gaines?" he asked with an accusing tone.

I looked him from head to toe. "I don't know. Fuck you asking me for?"

He got close to me. "This ain't no fucking game, Carl. Where is Bishop?"

I wondered if he knew I killed him. Fuck that. I wasn't admitting to nothing. "I just told you I don't know. Why you think I did something to Bishop? And how the fuck you find out where I live?"

"Because ain't nobody in this city stupid enough to kill a politician but you. He didn't go home last night. That's not like him. What did you do?"

I couldn't let him see me sweat, so I flipped the script. "Listen, man, I don't know where the fuck Bishop at, but he ain't up in here. You and yo' niggas need to get the fuck outta here before I lose my cool."

The old man's stare was serious. "You a stupid little dumb nigger. Not a nigga, but a nigger. You should've played ball. You shouldn't have taken it personal. Now you've unlocked some shit that you will wish you didn't." He stared at me again before shaking his head and leaving.

After they left, I closed the door and flopped down on the couch.

"What the fuck was that?" Tito asked.

I told the truth. "I don't know, brah. I really don't know."

J-Blunt

CHAPTER 2

After my run-in with Charles Brown, I kept my eyes open for the "shit that I unlocked". After two weeks with nothing happening, I went back to life as normal. Picking up money, dropping off dope, and running my club. The fucked up part about getting money was cleaning it. Kianna had fucked up Lace so I couldn't clean the money like I used to. Ended up stacking it in the trunk of my donk in storage again. The only bright spot was the five million that Lace cleaned for me. It was tucked away safely in an offshore account that I wasn't touching. That was my rainy day money. Never knew when I might need it. Until then I was going to stack my money and keep my eyes and ears open for another potential investor that didn't mind playing with dirty money. Besides, I had other shit to deal with. Like the lonely feeling that was starting to creep up on me and fuck with my head.

"Good morning, Carl."

I turned my head and seen pretty green eyes blinking rapidly. I couldn't remember her name, but she looked familiar. Like I'd seen her on TV. "What's yo' name?"

She looked offended. "Excuse me?"

"What the fuck is yo' name?" I snapped, not understanding what was so hard about the question.

"I'm Trisha Montgomery," she yelped, sliding back a little.

I let the name and face roll around my head a couple of times. She was the little honey dip from the tattoo reality show.

"Oh yeah. Trisha, right. Sorry about that. I'm not good with names. Excuse me," I said before climbing out of bed and throwing on a robe. After finding my phone, I left the room. Tito, Brandon, and Webbie were in the living room. "Somebody get that bitch out my bed and give her a ride home," I mumbled, heading for the kitchen.

"Aye, Carl, that's Trisha Montgomery in there. What you doing?" Webbie asked, looking at me like I lost my mind.

"For real, nigga. Get yo' ass back in the bed and go fuck the rest of the day away," Tito said.

I grabbed a bottle of Patron off the counter and poured myself a drink. "She don't know how to suck dick and the bitch snore," I said before downing the shot.

"I don't think you heard what my nigga just said," Brandon cut in. "That's Trisha Montgomery! She an up and coming boss bitch. Fuck with her. It's gon' pay off."

I poured another drink and slammed it. Then I looked at my security. "Why is that bitch still in my bed? "

Brandon moved towards my room. "I got it."

Tito and Webbie shook their heads at me. I waved my hand at them and pulled out my phone. After thinking of something to say, I called Shawn.

"Hello?" she answered with plenty of attitude.

"Did you hear from Kianna yet?"

"No, Carl. She don't want to talk to you, and neither do I. Would you please stop calling my phone?"

"C'mon, Shawn. I know I fucked up. Just put her on the phone. I need to talk to her. It's important."

"She not here, Carl. For real. She moved on and she don't want to talk to you. You put her in the fucking hospital, nigga. Leave us alone."

Click.

Visions of Kianna floated through my head as I stared at the phone. She was my ride or die. My black Bonnie. My Beyoncé. Spilled blood for me. Would've walked through fire for me. Loved me when I wasn't shit. And then I beat her ass and kicked her to the curb like a piece of trash. And now I missed her.

"Oh really, Carl? You can't even tell me to leave, so you have one of your boys do it for you?" Trisha snapped, walking from the room carrying her heels.

"I had a good time, but you don't know how to suck dick, so..." I shrugged.

She threw a shoe. "Fuck you, you li'l dick-ass nigga!"

The shoe missed me, but I still got pissed off. I grabbed the bottle of Patron and rushed her ass. She froze like a nigga trying to break into a store getting caught by bright-ass floodlights. I

22

snatched her by the hair, throwing her to the ground and dousing her with liquor. "Learn how to suck dick, bitch! And quit snoring."

When she started kicking and screaming, I let her go.

"Let me go! Fuck you, Carl! You gon' get yours, bitch-ass nigga!"

"Get this bitch outta here!" I snapped at Brandon.

It took all three of them to get her crazy ass out of my condominium. While my niggas dealt with the crazy VH-1 diva, I flopped down on the couch and thought about the one I let get away. I missed Kianna like I never thought I would. She understood me. Loved me. I could talk to her about real shit and get a good response. I needed that now more than ever. All those stupid-ass love songs about letting your girl get away started playing in my head.

And then my phone rang.

"What up, Chris?"

"It's all bad, brah," he lamented.

I pushed Kianna from my head and sat up. "What's going on, li'l brah? Talk to me."

"Somebody got Donovan last night. He gone."

I closed my eyes as the pain hit home. "Damn, that's fucked up. I'm on my way to the city. I'ma call you when I get there."

After taking a shower and getting dressed, I hopped in the Bentley with Webbie and Tito and made the trip to Milwaukee. Chris met me at Donovan's house. He hopped out of the Porsche truck looking like real money. Shiny bald head, trimmed facial hair, iced out TBT chain.

"What's good, brah? You been in there yet?" I asked as we embraced.

"Nah. I was waiting on you."

I nodded towards the house. "Let's get to it."

After ducking under the police tape, I used the key to let us in. The TV was still on, a plate of food on the table like he was about to eat. We walked to the hallway, but stopped at the puddle of dried blood outside the bathroom.

"Damn, Don," Chris mourned.

"Let's check on the money," I said, leading the way to the basement.

I kept money in different traps just in case I needed it. When I seen parts of the furnace strewn on the floor, I knew the money was gone.

"Not too many people knew about this."

"Just me, you, Bran, and Tone," Chris said.

"And Kianna," I added.

Chris gave me a look. "She wouldn't do this. She know how to get it."

"I know," I nodded. "Let's get outta here. Let everybody know what happened and put some money on the nigga head that did this. It was 100 G's in there so put 200 G's on they head."

Chris nodded. "I'ma put the word out."

"Let's go see Bran and Tone. You need a second in command. If they didn't have nothing to do with this, one of them gon' be yo' right hand. Catch a ride with me so I can holla at you."

After we were seated in the back of the Bentley, I called around and found the brothers. They were together at Tone's house.

"What's going on in the city?" Chris asked as we rode through the city.

"I'm moving from the condo. Thinking about a mansion out north."

Chris looked surprised. "You moving? Why?"

"Remember the Alderman I told you about?"

"Bishop Gaines's bitch ass." He nodded. "What happened? He came to the crib?"

"Nah, I popped his ass. But his nigga came to the condo asking questions. Said some shit about a billionaire's cartel."

"That shit real?" Chris asked skeptically.

"I don't know for sure. But if they is, I might've made us a new enemy."

"You need me to come back to the city and fuck shit up?"

"Nah, not yet. It's been a few weeks and I haven't heard nothing. But I'm still moving, just in case. I don't like niggas knowing where I lay my head at."

"Fa sho'." He nodded.

We were silent for a few moments.

"Anybody heard about Ki-Ki?" I fished.

Chris looked at me. "I didn't know you was looking for her."

I turned my head to look out the window so he wouldn't see the pain in my eyes. "I fucked up with her. One of them situations that you never know how much somebody mean until they gone."

"Damn, I never thought I'd hear my big brother going soft." Chris chuckled.

"Fuck you, nigga."

"I'm just bullshitting." He laughed. "But real shit, I'ma keep my eyes and ears open. Kianna was like my big sister. TBT to the heart. If I hear something, I'll let you know."

I nodded.

"I got a li'l thang that's tryna lock me down, too," Chris admitted. "Her name is Sheila."

That made me smile. "Don't tell me Cartier Chris getting soft on these hoes!"

He turned red. "C'mon, my nigga. I been pimping since pimping been pimping. But that nigga Lyfe said, 'When you find somebody good, you hold on to them'."

I thought about Kianna. "Yeah, sometimes them R&B niggas be knowing what they talking about."

***

After meeting with Bran and Tone, I decided to give Tone the slot under Chris. Bran would be next in line if needed. When that was squared away, I went back to the Windy City. As soon as my Bentley entered the city limits, I called Sergeant Snipes and set up a meeting.

"You find in anything about BBC?" I asked when he climbed in the backseat next to me.

"That shit like a secret society, Carl. Don't nobody that know about them speak about it. Everybody that I talk to, even the niggas that's plugged into the heart of the city, act like they don't know nothing. I ain't never seen no shit like this. Either they really don't exist, or they don't want nobody to know they exist."

I took a moment to think about what he said and remembered a quote I heard from a movie. "The greatest trick the devil pulled was convincing the world that he doesn't exist." BBC was the devil. Or they were some pussies.

"Okay. Let me know if you hear something. In the meantime, I need you to find me some loyal soldiers. I'm about to start a Chicago chapter of Triple Beam Team. What you got?"

The cop thought for a moment and then smiled. "Drive over to Foster Park."

When Webbie pulled the Bentley up to the park, Sergeant Snipes got out and began looking around. I got out and took a look with him. There was a physical basketball game in full swing. Groups of young niggas were in huddles on the sideline.

"Big Fred is the bald head one with the red shorts and no shirt," Snipes pointed. "He just finished doing three years in Joliet. Tank is on the bleachers with the gold dye in his dreads. He also just got out. And Hootie, the one by the light pole wearing the Bulls jersey, also just got out. They are your three prospects."

I took a long look at the three young niggas. There was nothing special about them. Big Fred was tall and the other two looked like every nigga in the hood. "How do you know them?"

The cop smiled. "I sent all they asses to Joliet."

I gave him a concerned look.

"They are my li'l niggas. Couple savages with no direction. I gave them some. They loyal soldiers. So loyal that they took a case for me and didn't say a word. I told them they wasn't gon' do that much time, and they didn't. They all did three years. I made sure they didn't want for nothing while they was in. Now they out and it's time for them to leave the nest and learn how to fly."

I chewed on his words for a moment. "They so loyal that they would do a bid for you, huh?"

"Good soldiers. I think of them like sons."

"Call 'em over. Let me holla at 'em."

The cop went to gather his sons, giving them all loving hugs. After a few words, he walked them over to me. Uncertainty shone in their young eyes as they watched me.

"Boys, this is my nigga, Carl. He wanna talk to y'all for a moment."

"'Sup, li'l niggas?" I nodded.

They nodded back.

"Y'all ever heard of Triple Beam Team?"

They exchanged questioning looks before Fred spoke. "Nah, I ain't never heard of it. What's that?"

"One of the best things that's gon' ever happen to y'all." I grinned.

J-Blunt

CHAPTER 3

I stood in my mansion on the north side of Chicago, basking in the beauty of three levels of 3,200 square feet. Cathedral ceilings, two living rooms with fireplaces, big-ass windows, a chef's kitchen, six bedrooms, seven bathrooms, a theater, a decked-out patio, pool out back, and a three car garage. All for 2.5 million dollars. I felt like a king. And tonight, after I closed the club, I was going to bring some bad bitches back to my new house and fuck like a porn star! But first, I had to take care of a small problem. After punching in my alarm code, I left the house and hopped in the backseat of the Bentley.

"Take me to the condo," I told Brandon.

We rode through the city listening to Meek Mill's song, "Cold Hearted", on repeat. That's how I felt. Cold-hearted. That's what it would take to finally end the cold war.

Brandon pulled the Bentley into the condominium's underground parking garage. We took the elevator to the fifth floor. I used the key to let us in and got smacked in the face by weed smoke. Big Fred and Hootie sat on couches, flanked by females.

"What's good, my niggas?"

"What up, Carl?" Big Fred grinned.

"You what's up. I see y'all having a good time. Where is Tank?"

"He in the room. Want me to get him?" Hootie asked.

"Yeah, grab him," I said before copping a seat. "So, what y'all think? Y'all like the crib?"

"Man, this is rich nigga shit, Carl." Big Fred nodded.

"Good. Good. Y'all niggas get used to this. I'm giving y'all this spot. It's a TBT world. Whatever we want, we get."

"Carl, what's good?" Tank asked, buttoning his pants as he walked into the living room.

"You got the best hand, my nigga. See you was in there doing yo' thang."

He smiled. "Yeah. Shorty a bad one."

"Fa sho'," I agreed. "Ladies, I need y'all to excuse us for a moment. Go in the other room while I talk to my niggas."

After the girls left, I addressed my young'uns. "I'm giving y'all a taste of what the Triple Beam Team life is about. You work hard and play harder. Me and my niggas don't want for nothing. We see what we want and then go get it. That's the Triple Beam way. I gave y'all a couple days to experience the life. Now I'ma give y'all the opportunity to be a part of this forever. Staying with the team involves work. You gotta carry yo' weight and put in work. Buss that thang. If you think that's too much for you, there go the door. But if you ready to live like kings, pledge TBT for life."

I paused to look in each man's eyes. And then I started with Tank. "What you wanna do?"

"It's a Triple Beam world, boss."

I looked to Fred. "Tell me something, big man."

"You already know. Triple Beam the only way."

I looked to Hootie.

"You don't even gotta ask me. Triple Beam Team til the world blow up."

I smiled like a proud father. "Welcome home, boys. The heavy lifting start tonight. Get dressed and let's go downstairs."

When we were in the garage, I led them to a black Nissan truck with tinted windows. "This the initiation, baby boys. Get in this truck and take a ride with Tito. Everything y'all need is inside. Y'all about to jump in the big leagues. Everybody in the house gotta die. Is that clear?"

Murder, eagerness, and the desire to prove themselves stared back at me. I knew the pups wouldn't let me down.

"It's done, Carl." Hootie grinned.

"Let's get it."

***

Revenge played in my head like a song I couldn't forget the words to as I rode in the back of the Bentley. When we turned onto the block where the killings would happen, I rolled down the window.

"Pull over right here," I told Brandon.

He pulled over a few houses away from the brown and white Victorian style house that sat in the middle of the block. The neighborhood looked peaceful, but in a few minutes, that would change. At 9:00 on the dot, the black Nissan truck turned onto the block. It parked in front of the brown Victorian and my three killers jumped out dressed in black. They moved with purpose up the walkway. Hootie held the screen door open while big Fred got a running start and smashed the door open. The killers raced inside. Shots rang out a few moments later.

Pop, pop, pop!

Silence for a few moments, and then more gunfire.

Pop, pop, pop, pop, pop!

The three killers left the house in a hurry, hopping into the Nissan and getting away. It took less than thirty seconds to knock off Alderman Charles Brown and his wife.

"Let's go, Brandon." I grinned.

***

Two days later, I was standing outside an apartment building on the south side of Chicago. Big Fred, Hootie, and Tank stood next to me. Brandon and Tito were sitting on the hood of the Bentley waiting for me. Sergeant Snipes and his partner stood on the stoop, listening to me give final instructions to the boys.

"This is where y'all starting at, but it's just the beginning. Snipes and Cooper gon' bring the money to y'all. Y'all won't even have to leave the building. Getting money is the name of the game. It's a Triple Beam world."

The boys nodded that they understood.

I turned to the cops and caught Cooper giving me a dirty look. "Something on your mind, nigga?"

He looked caught off-guard. "Me? Nah, Carl. We good."

I let my stare linger. Something about that nigga rubbed me the wrong way.

"C'mon, Carl. That's my boy. He good," Snipes spoke up, defending his partner.

I turned my attention to Snipes when I heard tires screeching. Two dark-colored vans stopped in the middle of the street. The doors were open and niggas dressed in black, wearing surgical masks, hopped out with machine guns. And then it went up. Brandon and Tito got hit first. They didn't get a chance to pull their guns before the niggas in the vans got down on them. Machine gun bullets sprayed the porch, forcing me to get down. I was reaching for my pistol when I seen the betrayal.

Sergeant Snipes and Cooper pulled guns. Snipes took aim at the niggas in the van. Cooper pointed his pistol in his senior officer's face and squeezed the trigger. Sergeant Snipes fell next to me, brains oozing out the side of his head. I grabbed my gun, ready to light Cooper's ass up, but he already had his gun on me.

"Point it at me, bitch, so I can blow yo' shit out!" he threatened.

I froze.

Cooper took my gun and snatched me up by the shirt. The other niggas with machine guns came and dragged me to one of the vans. I looked around and seen the ground covered with my niggas. Brandon and Tito lay in the streets bleeding. Tank, Hootie, and Big Fred were on the porch, dead. Then somebody put a bag over my head and the world went dark.

The van was quiet. Nobody said a word. I knew not to say anything because these niggas wasn't going to talk back. They were pros. Had to be ex-military by the way they moved. They crept up on us and killed all my niggas without us firing a shot. If they wanted me dead, they would've killed me. They wanted me alive. I was the mission.

About ten minutes later, I smelled water. We were near Lake Michigan. When the van stopped, I was handled roughly. Got dragged inside a building and thrown on the ground.

"Take the bag off his head," a man spoke.

The bag was ripped off my head. I looked up at six heavily-armed niggas dressed in black military clothes with masks on their faces. Cooper stood with them, a smug look on his face.

"What's up, Carl?"

The voice came from behind me. I spun around and locked eyes with a tall dark-skinned nigga that instantly reminded me of Denzel Washington. Looked to be in his early forties. Short curly hair, white smile, and slim build. Wore a tailored suit and loafers.

"Who are you?"

He squatted down so that we were eye to eye. "I'm Denzel Valentine. I see you met my boys."

I didn't know what to say. This nigga was actually real!

"I won't lie, Carl. You gave me a really hard time." He smiled, standing again. "You killed two of my best mouthpieces. Bishop Gaines was a good man. Charles Brown was a father to the city. You had him and his wife gunned down a couple nights ago. That was wrong. I should have your ass gutted and turned into shark food." He paused to stare at me for a moment, the decision to kill me playing in his head. "But I won't. Charles wanted you dead, but I'm going to spare your life. He said you were dangerous, but I see potential. Which is why you are here. If you look around, you can see that this is the same boathouse you killed Bishop Gaines in."

I was tired of hearing this nigga talk. "What you want, Denzel?"

He looked at me like he was attracted to me. "I want you, Carl. It's always been about you. And right now, I'm going to give you the opportunity to get even. "

He pulled on a pair of gloves before taking a gun from Cooper. He took the clip out leaving a bullet in the chamber. Then he set the pistol in front of me.

"You have one bullet, Carl. You can kill yourself. You can kill me and then be killed. Or you can kill the Judas that's been with you all along."

"C'mon, Denzel. What are you doing?" Cooper panicked.

"Shut up!" Denzel ordered. "So, what's it going to be, Carl? What do you choose?"

I picked up the gun, holding eye contact with Denzel. There wasn't a drop of fear in his eyes. I wanted to kill his ass, but that would've signed my death certificate. His soldiers would've put so many bullets in my body that it would've taken the medical examiner a week to get them all out. Plus, Denzel wanted me alive. And I really wanted to kill Cooper's bitch ass for setting me up. I lifted the gun to the cop's face and blew his brains out.

Denzel closed his eyes, nodding and smiling. "Thank you, Carl."

I dropped the gun. "For what?"

He picked the gun up. "For giving me what I needed. You just killed a police officer, brotha. I could turn you in and make sure that you never see the streets again. But that would be a waste of talent. So this is what's going to happen. From this point forward, TBT belongs to me. You work for me. All the money that you have in the trunk of your car is mine. The millions that hedge fund manager cleaned for you is mine too. And in return, you get to be a part of the greatest Black Mafia family the world never knew existed. Welcome to the Black Billionaires Cartel!"

CHAPTER 4
One month later

"So that's it? Some nigga named Denzel just come along and take TBT from us?" Chris yelled, slapping a hand on the table.

I was at his house in Milwaukee. Webbie stood by listening, shaking his head.

"You think I wanna give this nigga my shit?" I yelled. "I put blood, sweat, and tears into this shit. You know how many mutha-fuckas I had to kill to make sure Triple Beam Team made it? I sacrificed more than anybody. I put in more work than everybody. I am the founder of this thang!"

"And now you just gon' give it up?"

I thought about Denzel having the pistol with my DNA on it. "I don't have a choice. They got politicians, judges, and police. They even got they own bank. These niggas is way bigger, way stronger, and way more plugged. Either I play by they rules or get shut down."

"So what happens now?"

"Nothing changes. Everything stays the same. Dope prices still the same and everybody still get the same cut. The only change is at the top. I work for Denzel and we all under the BBC umbrella. Don't tell nobody about this conversation. Not yo' bitch, yo' best friend, nobody. Don't even mention it in your prayers when you talking to God. What I said don't leave this room. You got that?"

"Man, whatever," Chris sulked.

"I'm not playing, Chris. Don't say shit to nobody. Not one word."

"Like I'ma tell somebody that we got hoed outta our shit. I can't believe this shit."

We sat in silence for a moment.

"Have you heard anything about who killed Don?"

"Nah. Nobody talking."

"What about Kianna? You hear about her?"

"That's a no-go too. I had some shit to tell you about these Get Money niggas, but it don't seem important now."

I raised an eyebrow. "Get Money niggas? What the fuck is that?"

"They called Get Money Team. Niggas been moving weight on the north side. Starting to have little run-ins with our niggas."

"How long this been going on?" I frowned.

"The last situation happened a couple days ago. I'm tryna figure out who these niggas is. I got niggas looking into it."

The last thing I needed was some niggas trying to get in my pockets. Especially now that I had to start over. "Keep me up on the dealings with these niggas. Shut that shit down and don't let up. Shut that shit down!"

"I'm already on it, Carl. I got it."

"A'ight. I gotta get back to the city. Remember everything I just told you."

"I got it, brah. I got it."

A key being inserted into the front door made us pause. When it opened, a bad-ass exotic looking female walked in the house. She looked like she could be a Kardashian. She had brown and blonde hair in a ponytail atop her head that hung past her shoulders. Perfectly-arched eyebrows. Makeup on point with smoky cat eyes. Her skin was tan like she just came from vacationing in Florida. She had a beautiful face, and her body looked so perfect that a nigga would've thought she paid for all the parts. Titties wanted to bust out of the snug white T-shirt and the white leggings sculpted her hips, thighs, and ass like a second layer of skin.

"Hey, Chris. I didn't know you were having company," she said, switching over to give him a kiss.

"Hey, baby. This my brother, Carl, and our nigga, Webbie. They just came from Chicago. Aye y'all, this my girl, Sheila."

"What's good, shorty?" I nodded, trying not to stare. My little brother knocked a twenty piece!

"Hi, Carl." She smiled, extending a hand. "I've heard so much about you. It's nice to finally meet you."

I shook her French manicured hand. "It's nice to meet you, too. And honestly, I haven't heard enough about you."

She blushed, looking deep into my eyes. "I'm not going anywhere."

Chris mugged me. "Dawg, how you gon' flirt with my girl right in my face, nigga?"

I laughed at the show of jealousy. "I wasn't flirting, nigga. I was just being cool. You tripping."

"Sounded like flirting to me. Don't you niggas got something to do? Wasn't y'all about to leave?"

"Ooh wee! Got all in yo' chest." I laughed, heading for the door. "Aye, Sheila, you take it easy on my little brother. It was nice to meet you again."

"Cartier got him a bad bitch!" Webbie whistled as we walked to the Bentley.

I thought about the look she gave me. "Yeah. And she already wanna suck my dick."

Webbie frowned. "You tripping."

"What?" I shrugged. "I didn't say I was going to let her."

After we were in the ride, Webbie drove to the gas station to fill the tank before we hit the highway. I sat in the passenger seat, thinking about the get together Denzel was throwing. He said he had some people that he wanted me to meet. I didn't want to go, but I didn't have a choice. Couldn't upset the boss. Just the thought of having to answer to another nigga pissed me off. If I ever got the opportunity, I was going to kill that nigga.

I was having these murderous thoughts when a silver Benz pulled up to the pump across from my Bentley. I made eye contact with the woman driving. She looked to be around my age and her eyes were hard, telling about the rough life that she lived. She had light brown skin, her hair cut low with brushed waves. Something about her looked familiar, but I didn't give it much thought because Webbie was getting back in the car. He was about to drive away, but stopped.

"You know her?"

I turned to see what he was talking about. The short-haired woman was walking towards the Bentley. She wore a T-shirt and jeans, the blue denim showing a curvy body that could only be described as sturdy. She motioned for me to let down the window.

"Is your name Carl?"

I studied her face for a moment. I knew her, but didn't know how I knew her. "Yeah, I'm Carl. Where I know you from?"

Her eyes grew wide and she started laughing. "Oh my God! I can't believe it's you! What up, nigga? This Marie."

I searched my memory, trying to place the name and face. "Marie, Marie, Marie…" I repeated.

She put a hand on her wide hip and gave me that look. "I met you and Rideout at Sherry's house on your nineteenth birthday. In the bathroom. Minute man."

An image of fucking her on my nigga's sink twenty-something years ago popped into my head like a scene from a movie. "Oh shit! Marie, what's good?"

"Nothing, man. I'm okay. Last I heard, they said you was doing life in prison. What happened? When you get out?"

"I been put that shit behind me, baby. Been out since 2013. But look at you, riding around in a Benz. Look like you doing good."

"This is my son Drayez's car." Then her eyes grew wide. "I need to talk to you. Can I get your phone number?"

Even though we went way back, wasn't no way I was giving her my number. "How about you give me your number and I call you. I don't got a phone right now."

When she told me the number, I had Webbie put it in his phone.

"Okay, baby. I'ma give you a call," I said, letting my eyes roam over her body. "I see you still got it."

"Good genes." She blushed. "Make sure you call me."

"I will."

"She got a ass like a horse," Webbie said as we watched Marie walk away.

"Ole Marie." I smiled as memories of the old times played in my head. "She had some good-ass pussy. Made a nigga a Minuteman." I laughed.

***

I didn't get back to Chicago until after 7:00. The Black Billionaires Ball would be in full swing when I got there. Denzel wanted me to be there at 6:00, but I had purposely come late to show him that I didn't respect shit he had to say. The gathering was being held at a convention center. Security stood outside the door wearing black tuxedos. They looked like the Secret Service or Men in Black.

"What's your name?" one of them asked.

"Carlile White."

The other man checked the list on a tablet. "You're good. Who is he?" he asked, looking at Webbie.

"He's my security."

"There is no personal security allowed inside. We are your security. He will have to leave."

I thought about causing a scene to try and get my way, but I didn't think it would get me anywhere. Plus, these niggas looked like professionals. "Take a ride, Webbie. I'll call you when I'm finished."

After I was allowed into the building, I went through another checkpoint with a metal detector, where my pistol was taken and inventoried. Finally, I was allowed into the banquet area. It was a big-ass room filled with tables and chairs. Waiters dressed in black tuxedos walked around carrying drinks and food. There were about twenty security personnel posted in different places around the room watching everything and everybody. A live band was playing jazz music. There were about forty or fifty people standing around mingling. I didn't recognize anyone except Denzel Valentine. He was surrounded by a group of people, all the attention on him. He must've been telling a story, because the people around him seemed to be eating the words as they left his mouth.

And then he noticed me. He excused himself from the group and headed in my direction. The look in his eyes was serious.

"I'm glad you could make it, Carl." He smiled, draping an arm around my shoulder while leaning close to my ear. "And nigga, the next time I tell you to be somewhere at 6:00, you better be there at 5:59! I mean that shit. If you ever disrespect me or try to make me look like a fool again, I will forget about our deal and things between us will get real ugly. Do I make myself clear?"

I mugged the shit out of his ass, pushing his hand from my shoulder. "I ain't yo' bitch, nigga. I had some important shit to take care of. And I don't take kindly to threats. If you feel like you gotta do something, then do it. "

A fire lit in Denzel's eyes and he moved so close to me that our noses were almost touching.

"You testing me, boy? You think your dick is bigger than mine? You think all these rich, powerful, and influential people came here to see me or you? You think all this security is here to protect me or you? Who do you think runs this shit, me or you?"

We had another staring contest, neither one of us blinking.

"This is my chess game, Carl. I am the king. Everybody in this room does what I say when I say. Including you. Because of your disobedience, you just lost your liquor license at Triple Time for ninety days. Disobey me again, and I'm going to shut it down. Now let's try this again. Do I make myself clear? "

He stared me down, daring me to challenge him again. He wanted to strip me of everything and I couldn't let him do it. Losing my liquor license for ninety days was going to hurt my business. Nobody goes to clubs that don't serve alcohol.

"I hear you, man," I mumbled.

He took a deep breath as he backed away, satisfaction washing over his face like he had busted a nut. "I'm glad that we can be on the same page. Cooperation will get you everything, brotha. Insubordination will not be tolerated. Now, let me introduce you to everybody. These are some of the most powerful people in the city, Carl. The mayor, congressmen, senators, and Fortune 500 businessmen. This is the world you never dreamed you'd be a part of. And I just made it come true."

I moved around the banquet with Denzel, meeting the who's who on the Chicago power scene. The chief of police, The State's attorney, federal and circuit court judges. People I would've never met if it wasn't for Denzel. And I still hated that nigga. He was smug, arrogant, and self-centered. I couldn't wait until the day I could put a bullet in his face.

After shaking hands and giving fake smiles for an hour, I headed for the open bar. I was tired of sipping champagne and needed something stronger. As I walked across the room, it felt like someone was watching me. I searched until I found him. A short, light-skinned nigga with brushed waves, wearing a tan suit. He stood near a window on the other side of the room, holding a beer. We locked eyes and exchanged mean mugs all the way to the bar.

"What can I get you?" the bartender asked, interrupting my mean mugging match.

"Scotch. The older the better."

"I have Dewar."

"That's perfect." I nodded, turning to find the nigga in the tan suit. He was gone.

I took a quick look around the room, but couldn't find him. I would keep my eyes open though.

"There you go," the bartender said, setting my drink on the bar. "Let me know if you need anything else."

I grabbed the drink and took a sip while continuing to scan the room. I couldn't find the nigga in the tan suit, but I spotted Denzel poking his finger in the chest of a stocky bald headed nigga. The boss man's eyes were serious, his mouth twisted in displeasure as he spoke close to the man's face. The receiver of Denzel's wrath looked humiliated. He also looked familiar, but I wasn't sure why. After the heated exchange, the bald nigga headed for the bar.

"Bitch-ass fake-ass Denzel Washington looking-ass nigga!" he mumbled as he approached.

"What can I get you?" the bartender asked.

"You got some Hennessey back there? I need two glasses."

"One moment, sir," the bartender said before going to get the drink.

I eyed the bald nigga for a moment, trying to remember who he was. And then it hit me. He was Mikey Stokes. Back in the day, he controlled most of the West side Chicago.

"You Mikey Stokes, right?"

He turned to look me from head to toe. "What's up, Carl. See you got blessed in, huh?"

I chuckled. "That's what you call it?"

"That's what it is, brah. Welcome to the family."

The bartender set the drinks in front of Mikey and walked away.

"If this is a family, does that make Denzel our daddy?"

Mikey laughed. "Nigga sure think he is. Lousy muthafucka."

"So, what part do you play in this family?"

He took a sip and then gave an "aaah". "I'm your uncle."

I was surprised. "You and Denzel brothers?"

"Nah. We go way back though. Over thirty years. I helped him build this family."

I nodded, noting the disgruntlement in his tone. Somehow, I was going to use that to my advantage.

"So, Uncle. You think you could talk Pop into not taking my liquor license for ninety days? I'll make it worth your while."

He looked at me and then gave a smirk. "You wasn't playing by the rules, Carl. Insubordination will not be tolerated."

I needed to get Mikey in my corner and I was willing to do almost anything. "I have a proposal. If you do that for me, I will throw a party for you in your honor every Friday night for six months. I'ma call it Mikey's Friday Night Bash. Free drinks and plenty of bad bitches. It'll be all over social media. A party at Triple Time, the hottest club in the city, for you, every Friday."

Mikey looked impressed. "I tell you what. This is my counter offer; and it's nonnegotiable. Three months of Mikey's bash, and you gotta be my wing man when my side bitch's best friend, Rakesha, comes to town next week. Deal?"

I knew Rakesha was going to be a monster, but I needed Mikey. "You got a deal."

Mikey shook my hand. "Deal. I'll call you when Rakesha comes to the city. And by the way, keep your eyes on that nigga in the tan suit. His name is Darwin Hobbs, but we call him Duke. He was Charles's nephew. It's out that you killed his uncle and he wants blood. Me and Denzel told him that you're family now and that shit is dead, but you know how these youngsters are now days."

CHAPTER 5
Six months later

Being a part of BBC wasn't that bad. Yeah, it cost me millions of dollars, but the things I got in return were invaluable. Being a part of Black Billionaires Cartel came with a lot of perks, the biggest being the protection from people in high places. I could do just about anything I wanted in Chicago and get away with it. We also had our own bank so I didn't have to worry about finding ways to clean my money. Because Denzel had a steady supply of dope being shipped in, I was also getting my money back. Everything was going in my favor and every time I looked around, I was winning. Just like my Chicago Bulls were at halftime. I was sitting court wide at the united Center watching our star forward, Zach Levine, put on a show.

"Sheila wanna move to Atlanta. She got a call about being on a new show, *Married to the Game.*"

I turned to look at Chris as the words registered. "But y'all ain't married."

"I know. You know that shit don't matter. Only thing them producers care about is the drama and cat fights."

"What is this 'game' that she supposed to be married to? I know you ain't finna put them people in our business so yo' bitch can be famous? "

He looked at me crazy. "Hell nah! Not the dope game. The reality show game. You know that's the thing now. Everybody tryna get a show. See the same niggas and females on dating shows, Maury, and all them court shows. They tryna get them stories out there to see if some producer bite. Sheila want that TV money."

I laughed. "So you actually thinking about going along with that bullshit?"

He shrugged. "I'm thinking about it."

I laughed harder. "Let me find out you be holding her purse when you take her shopping, nigga. Fuck that reality TV shit. We getting real money. I need you in Milwaukee. Them Get Money niggas starting to be a pain in my ass. You supposed to been took care of that. And now you talking about moving to Atlanta. C'mon, brah. Where yo' head at?"

Chris was silent for a moment. I had hit a nerve. Good.

"They stronger than I thought," Chris spoke. "When we push, they push back. They smart and organized. Whoever calling the shots over there know what they doing."

I looked him dead in the eyes. "So what that supposed to mean? You don't know what you doing?"

He waved a hand, blowing me off. "I'ma take care of it, brah. I got it."

"You been sayin this for six months. When you gon' show me that you got it? Or do you need me to come fix it for you?"

We had a stare-off. Anger swirled in his eyes. "I said I got it. I'ma take care of it."

The anger and determination in his eyes was convincing. "Okay. Don't be blinded by Sheila's looks and that pussy. TBT is your first bitch."

We became silent.

"You figure out how to get us from under them BBC niggas?"

"I'm still working on it. I told you they plugged in. I met some of the VIPs that's plugged in Chicago. Judges, police chief, senators. They plugged, li'l brah. Breaking away will take time, thought, and patience. One wrong move will get me cooked."

"What if we can establish TBT in Atlanta?"

I shook my head. "You still thinking about Sheila and her TV dreams?"

He looked like he got caught stealing. "It ain't like that. Just hear me out on this. Atlanta is far enough away that we might be able to start over and go independent again. BBC controls Chicago, but not the whole world."

I gave his words some thought. "You already got the plane tickets, don't you?"

He laughed and looked towards the basketball court as players began coming from the locker rooms.

"What time does the flight leave?"

"Tomorrow at 3:00."

I shook my head. Sheila was getting in the way.

"You got three days, Chris. Be back in Milwaukee in three days. And while you down there, see if TBT can establish a foot on the ground."

After leaving the United Center, we hopped in the Bentley and headed for my mansion. During the drive, I got a call from Mikey.

"Big Mike! What's good?"

"You got it, brotha. How you doing?"

"Good. Just left the United Center after watching the Bulls beat Cleveland. Zach Levine is the truth!"

"Yeah, that boy is good, but the Bulls ain't going nowhere. We need to get real superstars that can dominate."

"Thanks for shitting on my dreams."

"I didn't mean it like that, but we gotta be real. Until we get a bonafide superstar, we ain't going to no championship. But that ain't why I called. I need your help."

"Last time you needed my help, I had to take a 300 pound bitch out to eat, drug her, and then have my security fuck her. I hope you don't need that kind of help again."

Mikey laughed. "Rakesha thinks that was you that fucked her and she swear she loves yo' light-skinned ass. But I don't need that kinda help. I need——"

Boom!

Something crashed into the Bentley, sending the phone flying from my hand as the world spun around. Airbags popped out, slapping me in the face. I was dizzy and dazed for a moment. After shaking my head a couple of times, I looked out the window and seen a banged up F-150 to our right. There was a van behind the truck and three niggas with choppers jumped out.

"Shit!" I cursed, grabbing my pistol. "C'mon, Chris! Move! They coming!"

Tat-tat-tat-tat-tat-tat!

Bullets tore into the side of the Bentley as Chris and I scrambled out the driver's side. Cartier pulled his pistol and we stayed low until the shooting stopped. When we locked eyes, we communicated without speaking. If we didn't fight back, these niggas was going to kill us.

"On the count of 3," I whispered.

"Wait! Look under the car to see where they at."

The nigga was a genius! We crawled on our stomachs and spotted three sets of feet walking to the car. Then we took aim and started shooting them in the shins and feet.

Pop-pop-pop-pop-pop!

The niggas went down screaming. When they were on the ground, we continued shooting until they were dead. I was getting up when the van pulled away. The driver wore a mask, so I couldn't see his face. But I knew those eyes. I lifted my pistol and emptied my clip at the van as it sped away.

"What the fuck was that?" Chris panicked, looking at the dead bodies.

"That was Duke's bitch ass," I grumbled, looking towards the Bentley. Webbie was laying against the driver's door dead, bullet holes filling his body.

"Who the fuck is Duke?"

"I killed his uncle," I said, trying to think of my next move. We just had a shootout in the middle of downtown Chicago and people were already recording us with their phones. Then I remembered Mikey Stokes.

"Help me find my phone!" I yelled, jumping in the backseat of the Bentley.

I found the phone on the floor. Mikey was screaming.

"Carl! Carl!"

"Yeah, I'm here."

"What the fuck was that? Was somebody shooting?"

"Duke just sent his niggas at me. They got my nigga, but we got them too. Duke got away."

"What the fuck! You sure it was Duke?"

"He wore a mask, but I know those eyes. It was him. And I'ma need some help. We downtown, and people recording us. The police on the way. Plus, I'm a felon."

"Okay. I'm about to call Chief Waters. Let the officers take you in and we'll have you out before the night is over."

I looked down the street as a patrol car sped in our direction with lights flashing.

"I need you to do me a favor, Mikey. Don't tell Denzel that it was Duke. I want to bust his ass myself."

***

Being plugged with BBC paid off in the best way. Freedom!

Chris and I were taken to Cook County, where we gave statements to the detectives. But instead of being put in cells with the gangsters, killers, and rapists, we were put in a conference room to await the chief of police. When Chief Joseph Waters showed up, we gave statements before being released to an awaiting Town Car. When I was resting comfortably in the soft backseat of the sedan, I breathed a sigh of relief. I looked over to Chris and seen him smiling from ear to ear.

"What you smiling at, nigga?"

"Brah, we just went to jail for killing three niggas with unregistered pistols in the middle of downtown and didn't do a minute in a cell. Now we riding in the back of a Lincoln on the way to your mansion. You sure you wanna give this shit up?"

It was my time to smile. The last time I had gone through Cook County Jail had been a totally different experience. I was treated like a nigga and sent to prison for almost twenty years.

"Why you smiling?" Chris asked.

"I was just thinking. Nah, we ain't leaving BBC. I'ma take it over!"

***

I spent the next couple days trying to track down Duke. Unfortunately, I couldn't find him. He had gone into hiding. But I would get his ass. I would never forget how he tried to knock me off and get the last laugh. As a result of the attempt on my life, Denzel Valentine sent me a new vehicle. He viewed me as a valuable asset and wanted to keep me alive to continue moving his dope. So when the grey Range Rover with tinted bulletproof windows showed up in my driveway with two combat trained bodyguards, Billy and Ren, inside, I didn't complain at all.

I was riding around the city in the backseat of my new bulletproof Range Rover when my phone rang. I didn't recognize the number.

"Hello?"

"Carl, this is Sheila. I think something happened to Chris."

I felt an instant pain in my chest. "What do you mean? Where he at?"

"I don't know. He didn't come back to the hotel last night and I'm worried."

"Did you try to call him? Did y'all have a fight or something?"

"No, we didn't fight. He was supposed to meet me at the hotel. I had a meeting with some TV producers, so we went our separate ways. When I got back to the hotel, he wasn't here. I've been calling him all night and all morning, but he didn't answer. His phone is turned off."

"Did you call the police?"

"They said they can't do anything for 72 hours. I think something happened to him. He was supposed to be here."

I tried to think of what to do, but my mind was blank and numbed by the thought of losing my only family.

"A'ight, I'ma try to get in touch with him. Let me call you back."

"Okay. If you find him, tell him that I love him."

After ending the call with Sheila, I called Chris's phone. It went right to voicemail, so I texted.

"You good, Carl?" Ren asked, noticing my distress.

"I don't know. I think something might've happened to my little brother."

"You need us to do anything?" Billy offered.

"Ain't nothing we can do from here. He in Atlanta."

48

"We might be able to get a flight on the boss's private jet," Ren said.

I was surprised. "Denzel got a jet?"

"Two," Billy clarified. "A G5 and a G6."

***

During the flight to Atlanta on Denzel's G5 private jet, I couldn't stop thinking about Chris. If something happened to him, I was going to be devastated. He was the only family I had. My mother killed Chris's twin along with my father and herself during a psychotic breakdown. My Nana died while I was locked up. I still had an aunt alive somewhere in Madison, but I hadn't talked to her in years. As I sipped Scotch from a crystal glass, my Nana's words about taking care of Chris played in my head like a broken record. If something happened to my little brother...

When the jet landed at the private airfield in Atlanta, I hopped in the waiting rental car with my security. During this drive to the hotel, I tried to contact Chris again. Still no answer. Then I called Sheila.

"Did you find him?" she answered hopefully.

"Nah, but I'm in Atlanta. On my way to the hotel. Meet me in the lobby."

When I walked into the Hilton, Sheila wasn't hard to find. She wore a white sundress and looked so good that she stuck out like Trump at a Black Lives Matter protest.

"Carl!" She waved, her body parts bouncing as she ran over. She wrapped her arms around me and squeezed, her body feeling like it belonged pressed against me.

"Hey, Sheila. Did you talk to any of the hotel staff? Do they have security cameras?" I asked.

She shook her head, tears in her eyes. "I haven't talked to anybody but the police. And I can't file the report until tomorrow."

"Okay, let me do some asking around. Go back to the room. I'll be up in a minute."

"I know this is a bad time, Carl," Ren said as we watched Sheila walk away. "But do she got a sister?"

"Or a mama?" Billy added.

I mugged both of them before heading to the front desk. A young Chinese woman stood behind the desk. Her name tag said Anne.

"Excuse me, Anne. Is the manager around?"

"Yes. Can I ask what the problem is?"

"My little brother was staying here, and now he is missing. I want to talk to the manager to see if he's heard anything."

Shock and surprise lit her slanted eyes as she picked up the phone. A few moments later, an older black man with a natural afro and thick mustache came from the elevator.

"I'm the manager, Steven Earl. You said something about a missing family member?"

I shook his hand. "My name is Carlile White. My brother, Christopher White, was staying here with his girlfriend. He didn't come back to the room last night."

"Um, okay. You know this is Atlanta. Lotta men come here and 'forget' to come home."

"Not Chris," I said seriously.

"And you ain't seen Sheila," Ren added.

"I can ask the staff if they've seen anything. Did you call the police?"

"They won't get involved for 72 hours," I said, looking around at the cameras. "Is there any way I could see the security footage?"

"Oh, no. Sorry, sir. Hotel policy. Only the police and staff."

"What if I gave you a thousand dollars?"

His eyes popped. "Cash?"

I pulled out a bankroll as thick as the Bible.

"Okay. Follow me. Right this way."

He led us into a room where several security personnel were monitoring cameras. The person is charge was a heavyset black woman wearing a bad lacefront wig.

"Margaret, I need you to show Mr. White the video footage from yesterday."

She looked me from head to toe like I stank. "Oh, hell nah! You know ain't nobody supposed to be in here, Steven. I ain't finna lose my job. Is you gon' pay my bills?"

I went in my pocket for more money. "I'll give you a thousand dollars."

She looked at the money, in my eyes, and back at the money again. Then the bills disappeared from my hand so fast that I didn't see her take them. "Tell me what floor and at what time. Some of the cameras were down yesterday, so we don't have everything."

I had to call Sheila to get the times and room number. It didn't take Margret long to find Chris, but the missing footage made it hard to put the entire puzzle together. She tracked him coming into the hotel a 9:56 p.m., but he didn't go to his room. He went to one of the floors where the cameras weren't working. Sheila came back later that night and was tracked to their room.

"So, we know that he came back to the hotel and didn't leave," Ren summarized.

"But somebody in this hotel knows something, because he didn't leave," Billy added.

"Can you rewind the footage a little more or check different angles?" I asked.

Margaret went to work, rewinding the footage and checking different cameras. Then I seen a face that I could never forget.

"Stop! Rewind that!"

Margaret did as I said.

"Pause it!"

It was the perfect moment. I could see Kianna's face clearly. Her beautiful brown skin, hazel eyes, and pretty smile. She looked happy walking in the crowd of niggas. A few of them wore GMT charms on their chains. I felt weak in the knees and had to grab the back of Margaret's chair.

"You know her?" Ren asked.

"Yeah," I mumbled. "I used to know her really well."

We stayed the night in the suite with Sheila. Every time my eyes closed, I was tortured by thoughts of Chris, Kianna, and Get Money Team. When the pain became too much, I went to the bathroom. As soon as I closed the door, the tears came. Chris was dead. I could feel it. Killed by rivals. I shouldn't have let him come to Atlanta. Somehow he ran into Get Money Team at the hotel and they killed him. What hurt more was the realization that Kianna was involved. Did she set him up? Did she pull the trigger? The more I thought about it, the more it burned and the harder the tears poured.

I cut on the shower and stepped beneath the stream, allowing the warm water to wash away my tears. Sometime later, there was a knock on the door. Before I could answer, the door opened and Sheila stepped in. We locked eyes through the foggy shower window as she walked over. She opened the sliding door and began staring into my eyes like she was reading my soul.

"He's gone, isn't he?" she asked, tears welling up in her eyes.

I couldn't say the words so I closed my eyes, thankful for the water washing away my tears. When I opened them again, I knew she understood because she began crying with me. We shared our love for Chris as well as the grief created by his death. Then she stepped into the shower, still wearing the sundress. She moved to stand under the water with me, our faces close enough to share a kiss.

"I don't know what to do," she whispered.

I searched her eyes for something to hold on to. I needed someone else's strength because losing Chris had taken all of mine. And in Sheila's brown irises, I found it. She needed something too. Me.

I kissed her lips while slipping the dress from her shoulders. It pooled at her feet, revealing a body that made me hungry. Perfect titties with brown areoles and rock hard nipples. Small waist, wide hips. She lay back against the wall and opened her legs, pulling me into her wetness. Her insides were as wet as the ocean and I dove in it until our pelvises were touching. Then I fucked her with every ounce of strength, pain, and mourning that was in my body. We cried for the loss of my brother as she gave me all of her and I gave her all of me.

CHAPTER 6

Five months had passed since the death of my brother and I still awoke every morning thinking about him. I missed the shit out of my nigga, and there was an open wound in my heart that wept for him every day.

I lay in bed staring at the ceiling, thinking about Kianna and Get Money Team. I still hadn't been able to track her down or rid myself of the GMT problem. Our beef was heating up and an all-out war was coming soon. They were digging into my pocket and had taken half of the city from me. Denzel was starting to notice my money shortage and started asking questions. I told him about GMT and that I was handling it. But I wasn't handling it. Shit was starting to get out of control. But I couldn't tell Denzel that. I had to take care of GMT. And Kianna.

"Oh shit!" I grunted, grabbing a fistful of Sheila's hair as she sucked the juices from my dick.

After I was drained, she kissed her way up my body, folding her arms on my chest and resting her chin on the back of her hands. We stared into each other's eyes for a few moments. In her twenty-six-year-old light brown eyes I seen only the desire to please me and make me happy.

"Good morning, Mr. White." She smiled.

"Good morning, baby girl."

"How did you sleep?"

"Good. You always make sure I sleep good."

She smiled again. "Good. You want me to make breakfast?"

"Sure. Something light."

She kissed my chin and climbed out of bed to put on a robe. "Come downstairs when you're ready."

When she left, I grabbed my phone to check the time. The doorbell rang. I had the Ring on my phone and was able to check the doorstep. Mikey Stokes waved in the camera.

"It's 8:00 in the morning, fool," I griped.

"I know. Get up. We need to talk. It's important."

I shuffled out of bed and into a robe. By the time I got downstairs, Mikey was already in the house, sitting on the couch in the living room.

"What's so important that you couldn't wait until a reasonable hour to come by my house?" I asked, plopping down on the couch across from him.

"Denzel wants to see you."

I waited for him to say more. He didn't.

"You couldn't have called or texted that?"

He shook his head, obviously irritated. "He wanted me to tell you in person and give you a ride."

"You mean to tell me that you drove all the way to my house in the snow just to give me a ride when I have my own cars and drivers? How much sense does that make?"

Anger flashed in Mikey's eyes. "I know how stupid the shit sound. I told him how stupid the shit is. I'm getting tired of this nigga treating me like an errand boy."

I seen an opportunity to sow a seed.

"Why don't you do something about it?"

He chuckled. "Denzel ain't tryna hear shit. He got the keys to the city. He thinks he a god and we all supposed to worship him and do his bidding."

"What if you could be in charge?"

Mikey gave me a sharp look, his eyes narrowing. "I don't want that," he whispered, looking around to make sure no one was listening.

"I think you are more cut out to lead us than him. You are more practical. A better thinker. You said it yourself: you helped him build BBC. This family might not be here today if it wasn't for you. You just as important as he is. He probably don't want you to realize that."

I watched the wheels turning in Mikey's head.

"Can't talk like that, Carl. That's dangerous, brotha."

"I know." I grinned, leaning back in my chair and holding his stare.

He switched the subject. "C'mon, man. Get dressed. I gotta take you to Denzel."

"What if I found a way to remove him that wouldn't get back to you? Would you help me do it?"

"C'mon, Carl. Chill, nigga," he said nervously. "We ain't finna go there. I gotta take you to see Denzel."

"Quit acting like Denzel's bitch and be yo' own man!" I snapped. "I fuck with you, nigga. I wanna see you shine. I believe in you. And I want to help you. If I can find a way to get him out of the way without it getting back to you, will you help me do it?"

Mikey held my stare for a long time. "Yeah."

I wanted to jump up from the couch and start dancing like Chris Brown, but I didn't. I just smiled. "Let me go find something to wear so I won't be late for this meeting."

***

After getting dressed, I hopped into the back of the Rolls Royce with Mikey. They took me to an indoor golf course, where I walked the greens and talked with Denzel.

"I have a 10:00 tee time with Governor Anderson, so we'll have to make this quick. Tell me about Milwaukee, Carl."

"Ain't much to say. That's TBT headquarters. Things is getting a little complicated."

He huffed. "A little complicated, huh? That's what you call losing millions of dollars in revenue? A little complicated?"

"Okay. Maybe it's a little more than that. But I'm taking care of it."

He stopped walking and turned to face me. "It doesn't seem like you're taking care of it, Carl. It seems like it's getting worse."

"I'm taking care of it, Denzel," I said firmly. "I got it."

He looked me from head to toe like I was a peasant. "Has losing your brother clouded your judgment or thinking in any way?"

I wanted to bust him in his shit. "My brother don't got nothing to do with this!" I mugged him, trying to control my anger.

"Still a touchy subject, huh?" He smirked.

I didn't respond. I had to bite my tongue to keep from cursing him out and whooping his ass.

"Listen, Carl. I brought you in because Triple Beam Team was making moves. I seen you as the next great leader and entrepreneur. Right now, I don't know who the hell you are. You are losing money and it doesn't seem to be pissing you off, but it's pissing me off. And if you don't do something about it, I will. Your seat at the table is dependent on your ability to pull your own weight."

He walked away like the arrogant and smug son of a bitch that he was, leaving me to chew on his words. And there was no mistaking his flavor. My relationship with BBC was dependent on me getting Milwaukee back under TBT control. And the only way I was going to be around long enough to knock Denzel off that high horse was to make sure I kept my seat at the table.

After finding Mikey, I had him drop me off at home. From my mansion, I had my security drive me to Milwaukee. It was time to step up the pressure on Get Money Team. When I got to the city, I called Bran and Tone and had them meet me at Midtown Shopping Plaza. Since Chris died, they were overseeing Milwaukee, and it was time to ramp up our attacks.

When Ren parked the Range, I spotted the brothers waiting for me outside the eyeglasses store. I hopped out on a mission. I was almost to them when Marie came walking out of the shoe store.

"Carl, what's up, nigga? Why you never called me?"

"Marie, hey girl. Listen, right now ain't a good time. We gon' have to catch up some other time. "

"Wait, Carl! Hold on. I'm not trying to hold you up. Just give me your number. I really need to talk to you. It's important."

Bran and Tone gave impatient looks.

"Okay. 555-8976. I really got something to do. Call me later," I mumbled before walking over to my niggas. "We need to get these Get Money niggas out the way, ASAP. We don't got no more time to play."

"I think that shit is already over with, Carl," Bran said.

I looked at him like he just told me my brother was still alive. "What you mean 'over'. What I miss?"

"We ain't heard nothing from them Get Money niggas in a minute," Tone explained. "Word is it had something to do with that nigga Diego getting knocked."

Now I was really lost. "Diego got knocked? When?"

"Feds did a sweep. Whole South side went up. Indictments galore," Tone said, his eyes wide with excitement.

The news was such a revelation that it shut my ass down for a whole minute. Now it all made sense. Diego had that good dope and enough of it to give me competition. When I started fucking with Denzel, Diego put Get Money Team on. Now that he was cooked, GMT was about to fade away. A dope boy is only as good as his plug. If he don't got a plug...

"Yeah, baby!" I fist pumped like Tiger Woods when he won that bitch-ass green jacket. "That is the best fucking news I heard in a long time!"

This brothers looked at each other and shrugged.

"So, what you want us to do? Slow down until the city cool off?"

"Just keep grinding, my niggas. Keep grinding," I sang, heading back to my bulletproof SUV smiling like I had just fucked Cardi B.

"That look say you just got some good news," Ren said.

"It's better than good news, my niggas. TBT is back! And as a matter of fact, I'm feeling so good that when Marie call me, I'ma tell her to give both of y'all some pussy."

"Is that the thick bitch you was just talking to?" Billy asked.

"Hell yeah. And that pussy is fiya!"

"Oh, hell yeah! I can't wait to get behind all that ass!" Ren grinned.

"Let's get back to the City, fellas. I gotta get another shipment from the boss!"

Hearing the news about Diego and GMT had me riding the best natural high I'd ever experienced. When my phone rang, I checked the number. I didn't know it.

"Hello?"

"Carl?"

Hearing her voice snatched me down from my natural high faster than a plane with engine failure.

"Kianna?"

"Yes. This is me. We need to talk."

So many feelings, thoughts, and emotions flooded my body that it was hard for me to concentrate. "What do you want to talk about?"

"My nigga, Drayez, wants to meet with you. We are Get Money Team. We want to discuss business."

CHAPTER 7

Kianna and her nigga wanna meet with me.

Kianna and her niggas are the founders of Get Money Team.

Those thoughts played over and over in my head as I sat at the table in Triple Time surrounded by my Triple Beam Team Niggas. The only woman that I ever loved helped someone rise up against me. And they also killed my brother. To hear her talk about her nigga and GMT burned in my body like my bone marrow was on fire. Her sins were unforgivable.

"The 750 Benz just pulled into the parking lot," Billy said, sitting next to me in the booth.

I nodded, choosing to remain silent so I could focus on keeping calm. A few moments later, I got my first glimpse of the leaders of GMT. Even though I had never seen Drayez, I knew who he was as soon as I saw him. He stood about 6'2" and 200 pounds. Caramel-skinned. Walked with the swagger and confidence of a boss. I could tell that having my girl and being in my presence was boosting the fuck out of his ego. He locked eyes with me the moment he walked in and maintained eye contact all the way to the table. Kianna walked beside him looking like the perfect boss bitch. Red dress, heels, hair and makeup popping. I didn't pay the albino nigga no mind. He really didn't matter. The meeting was about Drayez and Kianna.

"GMT in the building!" I announced as they approached the table.

"What up, Carl?" Drayez nodded, all cocky and full of himself.

"It's a real pleasure to meet the young nigga that's putting a dent in my pocket. And now that I see you, I can see why Kianna chose you," I said before looking to my ex. "You did good, Ki-Ki."

Kianna's face showed no emotion.

"I've been looking for you, Ki-Ki. Did your sister tell you?"

"Listen, Carl," Drayez cut in. "She with me now. I know y'all got history, but she my present. I wanna keep this between us."

The young nigga's arrogance, poise, and audacity surprised me. Couldn't believe he was in my club, surrounded by my niggas, but still not intimidated. The kid had nuts.

"Y'all have a seat. Mind if I call you Dray?"

"That's cool." He nodded as they sat.

"I gotta be real, Dray. When Kianna called and said you wanted to meet me, I was shocked, for two reasons. The first being that my lady had a new nigga and this nigga wanted to meet me. Second, this nigga that's putting a dent in my pocket got the audacity to want to meet me! I thought you was crazy or suicidal. You know how deadly this game can be. But now that you're here, I can see that you not crazy. You're ambitious. A young boss and deep thinker. Remind me of me. I believe in strong first impressions, and had yours not been impressive, that 750 you pulled up in wouldn't have made it back to Milwaukee. I hope you don't take as a threat, because that's not what it is. I told the truth because I respect you."

"Nah, I don't take that as a threat. I knew it was a possibility, and it was a risk I was willing to take. But I hope you wasn't gon' rest in that and think that my death wouldn't be avenged. Since we being honest, let me keep it real. I got a hit squad not too far from here. Some niggas you know. Trav n'em. I told them if I didn't come out of here to burn it down. And you know Trav can bring it."

Visions of my ex head of security popped into my head. That's why my niggas had problems getting rid of GMT. Trav. Just knowing that Trav was out there sent a chill up my spine. He was a beast.

"So that's what Trav is up to these days. You got a good one there. I hated to let him go. But here's a jewel. A general should pick his army well, both for skill and loyalty. Once a weapon is made, it can't be allowed to turn back on its user. Power must be delegated carefully. The blood of generals killed by their own lieutenant's fills many rivers. Many victories have turned to defeat at the hands of fucked up lieutenants."

I watched Drayez process the information. The seed had been sown.

"I hear you, Carl. But I'm not here to talk about Trav or armies. I wanna talk business."

"I guess we should get on with it, Dray. What's on your mind?"

"I need a new supplier. I don't know if you heard, but Diego got knocked. That was my man. Even though you my competition, I know you smart. This is an opportunity. How often do rivals set aside beefs and come together to do great things? Not often enough. Too many egos. But I'm settin' mine aside because I got a team to feed. Loyal soldiers need loyal generals. I love GMT. I built it and I wanna see it shine. The way I see it, this is a win-win. We can take over all of Wisconsin. A few power moves in different states and we can take over the Midwest. I'm proposing a TBT/GMT merger. We can be the Chrysler/Dodge of the streets."

When Drayez finished speaking, I considered the proposal. TBT/GMT didn't sound bad. I could bring more money into Black Billionaires Cartel and secure my seat at the table. Or I could kill Drayez and watch GMT fade away. They didn't have a supplier, and if I took out the leader, the clique would never recover. And then there was my brother, Chris. Drayez and Kianna were in Atlanta when he went missing. I needed to know.

"I hear you, Drayez. Since you've come into my club, you haven't disappointed me yet. I can't remember meeting somebody for this first time and thinking so highly of them. But before I respond to your proposal, I have a question. And this is serious; make no mistake about it."

He remained quiet, waiting for me to speak.

"About six months ago, my brother came up missing in Atlanta. He disappeared and his body hasn't been found. I did some digging and found out your team was in Atlanta around the time he went missing. I guess y'all made an impression because people remembered GMT. Now tell me it was a coincidence that GMT was in Atlanta when my brother came up missing. Tell me, Drayez."

I was so eager to hear his response that I leaned forward on my elbows, staring into his eyes like I was trying to read his soul. Drayez met and held my stare, never blinking or wavering. "I didn't know you lost yo' brother. I was in Atlanta a little while ago partying for my nigga's bachelor party. And yeah, we did it big. We always do. But I never met yo' brother. Us being in Atlanta at the same time was a coincidence."

I watched him intently as he spoke, looking for signs of dishonesty. The little nigga was a good liar. His body language didn't betray him. But I knew he was lying. And I didn't believe in coincidences.

"Okay, Drayez. Call it a coincidence. Now as far as business goes, I like it. But I will agree to the merger only on one condition."

"Name it."

I turned to Kianna. "I made a bad decision when I let her go. My ego got too big and I acted like a fool. My one condition is that you give me my girl back."

He looked to Kianna. "I owe this to the team, Kianna, but it's on you. What you wanna do?"

"Drayez, we built this together. I——"

"Leave, Drayez," I cut in. For my plan to work, I needed Kianna. "Leave right now and let her stay. Find a hotel to stay for the night and I'll get with you in the morning to make plans for the drop."

After taking one last look at Kianna, he got up and left.

"You want me to kill him?" Billy asked.

"Nah. Let him live for now." Then I turned my attention to Kianna. "We got some catching up to do."

We walked to my office in silence. She sat on the edge of my desk. I closed the door and leaned against it. We stared at each other for a moment. "So, Drayez is supposed to be a younger me?"

"If that's what you want to call him, yeah."

"You love him?"

"I don't love no more, Carl. It makes us weak. Ain't that what you said?"

"You remembered, huh? I told you that right before I fell in love with you."

"You also promised that you wouldn't hurt me. Then you and Donovan beat my ass and left me in the street bleeding," she said, a fire of hatred burning in her eyes.

"That was you that killed Donovan, huh?"

"He hit me. Plus I needed some money. Two birds with one stone."

"You sound cold."

"You made me this way."

"What about Chris? What he do?"

She twitched. "That wasn't me. I loved Chris. He was like my brother."

"Was it Drayez?"

She twitched again. "No."

"How you find out about Chris?"

"On Facebook."

I watched her again. "You love Drayez, huh?"

"I just told you, I don't do love."

"Then why are you lying for him?"

"I'm not lying."

We stared again. I walked over, lifted her chin, and kissed her. "I want you back. So much has happened since you left. Do you still love me?"

She searched my face, her eyes getting misty. "I never stopped."

"Will you prove it?"

"How?"

"Kill Drayez."

She twitched. "Why? He will make you a lot of money."

"Because money isn't everything. Because Get Money Team is a snake. To kill a snake, you gotta cut off its head. Drayez is the head. I told you this world ain't big enough for you to have two lovers. You created him. You gotta kill him."

Tears threatened to spill from her eyes until she closed them. When she opened them again, her eyes were clear. "Okay."

I kissed lips again. "Do you still love me?"

"Yes."

"Say it."

"I love you, Carl."

"You know what you have to do. Take care of that."

Kianna got up from the desk and walked slowly out of my office.

I gave a victory smile as I grabbed the bottle of Scotch and poured a drink. Revenge was a sweet-tasting bitch!

My phone rang. I didn't know the number.

"Hello?"

"Carl?" a woman questioned.

"Yeah. Who is this?"

"This Marie. You got a second?"

"Oh, hey Marie! Yeah, I gotta second. What you been up to all these years?" I asked, bringing the glass to my lips for another drink.

"I've been raising our son."

I never took that drink. "Say what now?"

"That's why I've been trying to talk to you. We have a son. His name is Drayez."

I dropped my glass. "Aw shit!"

BOOK II: ULTIMATE SACRIFICE

SACRIFICE - A THING GIVEN UP.

THE ACT OF OFFERING THE LIFE OF A PERSON, ANI-MAL, OR OBJECT IN PROPITIATION TO A DEITY OR GREATER CAUSE.

THERE COMES A TIME IN EVERY PERSONS LIFE WHEN YOU ARE FORCED TO MAKE A DIFFICULT CHOICE.

YOU MAY HAVE TO GIVE UP SOMETHING YOU LOVE IN ORDER TO KEEP SOMETHING YOU CAN'T AFFORD TO LOSE.

IN SOME CULTURES, PARENTS SACRIFICED CHIL-DREN TO PLEASE THEIR GOD.

IN THE STREETS, SOME NIGGAS GET KNOCKED AND SACRIFICE THEIR REPUTATION FOR A LIGHTER SEN-TENCE.

WHATEVER DECISION YOU ARE FACING, YOU MUST REMEMBER THAT ONCE A BULLET IS FIRED, IT CANNOT BE PUT BACK IN THE GUN.

PRAY THAT YOUR CONSCIENCE IS STRONG ENOUGH TO ACCEPT THE CHOICE LONG AFTER THE DEED IS DONE.

J-Blunt

CHAPTER 8
Drayez

I had just hung up the phone from Facetiming with Desiré when there was a knock on the door.

I immediately got on point. Was Carl trying to set me up, or is this how he did business? I wasn't sure, so I grabbed my pistol and crept to the door. Through the peephole, I could see Kianna standing in the hallway. *Fuck is she doing?* I wondered, unlocking the door. I hoped she wasn't mad that I left her because I didn't feel like arguing.

"Kianna, what the——"

She forced her way into the room, kissing me and making me swallow my words. I pushed her off.

"What the fuck you doin'?"

"I needed to see you one last time."

I checked the hallway before locking the door. "We made a deal. What if Carl finds out?"

"He won't."

"So what are you doing here? You mad that I left you?"

"No. You did what you had to do. It was a business move. It was best for GMT. I get it and I'm not mad. I didn't come to talk, Drayez. This might be the last time I ever see you and I don't want to spend it talking."

She pulled the dress over her head and let it fall to the floor. She wore a red bra, no panties, red bottoms, and the .380 strapped to her thigh. She looked sexy as fuck. Before I could decide what to do, she closed the distance between us and kissed me. I dropped the pistol and went with the flow. My boxers came off so fast that I didn't remember taking them off and we fell onto the bed, me on top. My dick was harder than a nigga in jail watching Beyoncé do a strip tease. Her legs wrapped around my waist, the .380 digging into my side. I grabbed it from the holster and threw it on the bed. When I pushed my dick inside, she gasped, biting my bottom lip.

"Yeah, Drayez!" she moaned. "Fuck me like it's the last time."

I went deep into her guts, long stroking and digging her out. She wanted more and rolled me over, never missing a beat as she rode me hard. I sat up to suck her titties and that made her ride faster. I grabbed her ass and squeezed, pulling her into me. That's when I felt something drip onto my forehead. I ignored it and kept sucking her titties until I felt it again. I looked up and seen Kianna's face wet with tears and sweat. This wasn't like her. The only woman I knew to cry during sex was Desiré.

"You good?"

She stopped riding, wrapping her arms around me, face in the crook of my neck. "I love you, Drayez."

Get the fuck outta here! The words stunned me. Why was she telling me this now?

"I didn't want to love you. I tried to hide it, Drayez. Tried to fight it, but it kept growing."

I tried to figure out why she was telling me this now. The deal was already made and I wasn't going back on it. This was about the team.

"I'm not telling you this because I want you to change your mind. I'm telling you this because I want you to know this is hard for me."

I felt the cold steel press against my temple. Nah! This wasn't happening! My hands was still palming her ass and I couldn't get to the gun before she pulled the trigger. If I flinched, she would kill me. I had to stay calm and buy myself some time.

"Carl doesn't want to make the merger. He thinks you are the head of the snake. If he kills you and takes me, he knows GMT will fall apart. He wants to eliminate the competition. He also can't accept the fact that I was yours. This world isn't big enough for me to have two lovers. This is why I didn't want you to meet Carl. I knew it would come to this. That's why I couldn't help you make the choice. It wasn't up to me. Your life was on the line. If we would've left the meeting without making the deal, I would've remained loyal to you. I would've remained your bitch and GMT."

While she was talking, a million thoughts ran through my head. It couldn't be over. I just wanted to make this last deal. I was looking out for the team. Why didn't Carl want more money? I answered my own question. Because money isn't everything. There are more important things in this world than money. Like principles. Morals. Integrity. Faith. Family. Love. And time. Time is more valuable than money. It was as clear to me now as it was when I was watching the doctors work on Draya in the emergency room. Van's words played in my mind. He said there would be a time in my life when I wished I could go back and do it all over. He was right. I wanted to hit the reset button. Time is this currency of life and my time was running out. I had to do something. Draya needed me. Junior needed me. Desiré needed me. Tikka needed me.

"I'm sorry, Drayez. You are my creation. I have to be the one to take you out."

I made my move.

The gun went off as I threw Kianna's ass on the floor.

Pop!

I climbed on top of her and wrestled the gun from her hand.

"Bitch, I should kill you! " I screamed, pointing the gun in her face while checking my head for blood. She didn't shoot me. Thank you, God!

"Kill me! I don't want to live!" she cried, closing her eyes and waiting for the blast.

I wanted to shoot her ass so fucking bad, but I couldn't. I had killed one of my closest friends, but I couldn't shoot Kianna. I continued kneeling over her with the gun pointed in her face. Banging on the door grabbed my attention.

"Drayez, you good?" Damo called from the hallway.

"Get dressed," I told Kianna before putting on boxers and opening the door.

Damo stood in the hallway holding a pistol. "You good, nigga? I thought I heard shooting."

I stepped aside to let him in. "Carl sent Kianna to kill me."

Damo looked stunned. "That was the gunshot?"

"Yeah. Watch her while I get dressed."

"I couldn't do it, Drayez. I told you that I love you," Kianna cried, wiping tears from her face.

"Bitch, you just put a gun to my head and pulled the trigger. I ain't tryna hear that love shit. Matter of fact, don't say nothing else to me. Shut the fuck up."

"So what's the move, brah? What we doing?" Damo asked.

"The first thing we gotta do is get the fuck outta this hotel. Carl don't wanna fuck with us. He wants GMT dead. He probably got niggas outside waiting for us or following her. I'm calling Trav and telling him to meet us outside."

Damo looked at Kianna. "Damn, Ki-Ki. What the fuck, shawty? What's going on?"

"Carl knows Drayez killed Cartier. He wanted me to kill Drayez, and when I went back to him, he was probably going to kill me."

"You couldn't have started with that shit? You had to pull a gun on me and almost kill me?" I snapped while dialing Trav's number.

"What's up, Dray?"

"It's a set-up, Trav. Meet me in the parking lot right now."

"Aw shit! Say less. I'm on the way."

After grabbing our shit, we left the hotel. I kept Kianna in front of me as we walked across the parking lot. If Carl was trying to set me up, I was going to use her as a shield. Trav, Fantasia, and a nigga from the hit squad named Bosco met me at my 750.

"What happened?" Trav asked in deep whisper as we searched the parking lot for anything that looked out of place.

"It was all a set-up. Carl sent Kianna to kill me and she almost did it."

Fantasia's eyes popped as he looked to Kianna. "Kianna! Bitch, I know you didn't!"

Kianna looked away in shame. "I didn't do it."

"But she thought about it!" I raised my voice. "Put the pistol to my head and pulled the trigger."

Trav shook his head. "Damn, baby. You savage."

"If I wanted you dead, Drayez, you wouldn't be standing here right now. I shot at the wall. I missed on purpose."

I exploded. "You shouldn't have put the muthafuckin' gun to my head in the first place, bitch!"

"Chill, Drayez. You have to deal with that later," Fantasia said. "Right now, we gotta get the fuck outta here. Carl might got niggas waiting for us."

Everyone began looking around after Fantasia's words.

"A'ight, y'all. Check it out. Bosco and Damo, y'all drive the 750 and take Kianna back to Milwaukee. Go to the auto salvage and stay there until I get there. I'm riding with Trav and Fantasia. Let's go bring that heat to these bitch-ass niggas."

Trav smiled. "I love watching you turn into a gangsta, li'l nigga."

I hopped in the passenger seat of the black Jeep Wrangler while Trav drove us back to Triple Time.

"What kinda heat y'all bring?" I asked.

Trav took his eyes off the road to wink at me. "Got some shit you ain't never seen before back there. Show him my bitch, li'l brah."

Fantasia reached behind the back seat and brought out a case that was almost as wide as the entire truck. He lay the case on the backseat and popped the top. Inside was a rocket launcher. I had never fallen in love with a weapon until that moment.

"I call her Hell's Angel." Trav grinned.

"Damn, this muthafucka is beautiful." I whistled, stroking the weapon of destruction.

"How you wanna play it, Dray?" Fantasia asked.

"I wanna drop as many Triple Beam niggas as possible before blowing Carl's shit back."

"We don't even know if Carl still in the club, and we probably ain't gon' make it through the front door," Trav said. "I say we send a rocket through that bitch and whoever don't die from the blast, we knock 'em off when they run outside. We got two ARs back there with hundred round drums. That's enough power to start a little war."

"Or end one." I smiled.

When we pulled up to Triple Time, Trav parked the Jeep in the middle of the lot and kept the engine running. I grabbed the rocket launcher while Trav and Fantasia grabbed choppers. We left the truck in a rush. There were four security guards outside the front door. Trav and Fantasia cut them to pieces.

Tat-tat-tat-tat! Tat-tat-tat-tat-tat-tat!

All of the niggas went down in a row. I walked into the middle of the lot and put the rocket launcher on my shoulder. After aiming it at the building, I squeezed the trigger. The rocket popped as it launched from the barrel and the gun kicked, pushing my shoulder and forcing me to take a step back to keep my balance. There was a loud whistle as the rocket flew towards the building, leaving a white trail of smoke. The projectile picked up speed before crashing through the front window. A moment later, there was a bright flash and loud boom. The building didn't blow up like explosions in movies, but all the windows shattered and the building caught fire.

"Damn," I mumbled, surprised at the destructive power of the rocket.

People began screaming as then ran from the building. Trav and Fantasia gunned them down. They dropped eleven or twelve bodies before the clubgoers realized they were being killed as they stepped outside. And when they stopped coming outside, we hopped in the Jeep and smashed out.

***

Three hours later, Trav parked the Jeep outside the auto salvage and we went inside. Damo, Kianna, and Bosco were sitting at the table.

"Y'all get that bitch-ass nigga?" Damo asked.

"I don't know. But we fucked them niggas up," Fantasia said, setting the ARs on the table.

"And this bitch performed beautifully!" Trav said, kissing the rocket launcher.

I watched Kianna for a moment. She didn't seem to care about what happened. When she noticed me watching her, she walked near me.

"Drayez, can we go somewhere and talk?"

I shook my head. "I don't got shit to say to you. You tried to kill me."

She got loud. "I didn't try to kill you, Drayez! Stop saying that shit."

"What the fuck you call it then? You was tryna scare me?"

"No, Dray. I didn't know what I was doing. I was trying to figure it out. You left and Carl told me what to do. I was confused. But I'm not anymore. I know where I belong, and it's with you and GMT."

I stared at her for a moment. Kianna was a bad-ass boss bitch. My partner. I would've done anything for her. She helped me reach a level in the game I never thought I'd reach. But I could no longer trust her. She thought about killing me. That was unforgivable.

"Whatever we had is over, Kianna. If you really loved me like you say you do, you should've come in the room and told me the move off top. It shouldn't have taken you putting a pistol to my head for you to figure that shit out. I don't know what you gon' do, but I'm done. Do you."

She grabbed hold of my hand, tears spilling down her face. "Drayez, please, baby! I didn't mean it. I'm sorry!"

I snatched my hand away. "Don't touch me no more and stay the fuck from around me."

She wrapped me in a hug. "Please, Drayez! Don't do this."

I looked to the muscular GMT hit squad member. "Fantasia, come get yo' girl off me."

"C'mon, Ki-Ki. Let him go, girl," Fantasia said gently, pulling her off me.

"Drayez, don't do this. I'm sorry. Please."

I didn't even acknowledge her words. Instead, I turned to my niggas. "Listen, y'all. I went to Chicago with a plan. I wanted to hook up with Triple Beam Team and get us a plug so we could get back to eating. I was going to turn everything over to Damo and her so I could be with my family. I just found out I got a son. I want to be there to raise my kids. But this shit with Triple Beam Team just got real. We gon' have to set this money aside and take care of these niggas because they want us gone. And I'll be dammed if I'ma let that happen. So for right now, all GMT hustling is on hold. It's a war. I need all hands on deck and in war mode. Let's put all these bitch-ass Triple Beam Team niggas in the graveyard.

CHAPTER 9

I left the auto salvage with Damo and Bosco and a lot on my mind. I needed to kill Carl, feed my team, and decide what to do with Kianna. And right now, all that seemed harder than solving a Rubix Cube.

"This shit so fucked up, Dray," Damo sulked as we walked to my Benz.

"Who you telling, my nigga? Soon as a nigga try to leave, something pulls me back."

"You was really going to leave the game?"

I didn't speak again until we was all in the car. "Desiré, my son, and my daughter pulling me out. I got a Junior, brah. I want to be there to raise my kids. But this shit tonight..." My words trailed off as I backed the Benz out of this driveway.

"So what's the plan now, brah? You know I'm riding with you all the way to the end."

"Right now, killing Carl at the top of the list. GMT ain't been hustling since Diego got knocked. It kinda seems like the ride might be over with anyway. If I don't find a plug, we through."

"And what about Kianna?"

I let out a long breath. "I should've left that bitch's brains on the hotel floor in Chicago. But one thing is for sure, I'm done fucking with that bitch."

"It's probably good that you didn't murk her. We can use her to get close to that nigga. She still knows how that nigga move. She was his bitch. She knows how he thinks. Then, after we use her to slump Carl, I'll blow her shit out for you."

I nodded. "That don't sound like a bad idea. Right now I need to make sure Desiré and the kids safe. We can figure out there rest tomorrow. We blew up his club and flamed up a lot of his niggas. That put him on notice that we ain't fucking around."

When we got to Desiré's apartment, I used the key to let us in. Damo and Bosco waited in the living room while I went to get Desiré and the kids. They were all asleep in her bed.

"Desiré, wake up, baby," I called, turning on the bedside lamp.

She must've heard the edge in my voice because she awoke looking concerned. "Drayez, what's wrong?"

"Pack the kids some stuff and let's go. We gotta leave your apartment. It ain't safe."

Her eyes grew wide as she sat up in bed. "I thought you were done? What happened? Tell me what's wrong."

"I can't right now. I'll tell you later. Get up."

She grabbed my arm. "No, Drayez. Hell nah! What the hell is going on? Tell me right now."

I searched her eyes and seen a will and determination that demanded the truth. So I told her.

"I was about to give it up, baby. I just wanted to make this last move and then it was gon' be me, you, and the kids," I said, having a vision of Kianna with the gun to my head. "Kianna betrayed me. She switched sides and almost killed me. Now I gotta finish it. But first I need to make sure y'all safe."

Desiré climbed out of bed, pressing her warm soft body against me, wrapping me in a hug. "Please, Drayez. Let it go and leave with me. Let's take the kids and go. We can go anywhere."

"It's not that easy, baby. People want me dead. It's a war. I gotta take care of this and I need you and the kids safe at my house."

Her eyes popped. "Your house? Kianna probably told them where you live. We not going to your house. We should leave the state."

"Kianna didn't tell them where I live. Plus, my people can protect you better at my house."

"How do you know she didn't tell nobody where you live? Is she dead?"

"No, she's alive. I got my people watching her. Listen, we can talk about this later. Right now I need you to get the kids ready."

She pushed me. "We're not going to your house. No. Especially if Kianna is still around. Hell no!"

She was pissing me off. "What the fuck is wrong with you? Can't you see that I'm tryna keep you safe?"

She walked in my face, anger lighting her eyes. "I'm not taking my babies to your house. If you don't like it, oh well. I'm going to my mother's house. Don't nobody know where she lives."

I was tired of arguing. "Okay. Pack y'all shit."

***

I spent the night at Desiré's mother's house with her and the kids. Everything that happened during the last couple of days had me mentally, physically, and emotionally drained, but I couldn't sleep. I lay in bed with my family, staring up at the ceiling as my thoughts ran wild. Kianna betrayed me, my team was starving, and I was in a war. I didn't know if I would make it out of this alive. There was also the possibility that I could lose my freedom. So much was on the line. I had a lot to lose. But I still couldn't walk away. Not until Carl was dead. That was the only way GMT would have a chance.

Later that morning, I met with the heads of GMT and the hit squad at the auto salvage to discuss our next move.

"A'ight, y'all. Everybody know the situation. These niggas want us gone, and we ain't folding. I need everybody in war mode and ready. We need to come up with a plan to bring it to these niggas," I said before looking to Kianna. "You used to fuck with that nigga. Tell us what you know."

She looked out on the spot. "Carl don't really got no family, so we can't use them to get to him. His momma killed his daddy and little brother, and you killed Chris. His granny died while he was locked up. He never lived in Milwaukee because he didn't want to shit in his own backyard. He used to have a condominium downtown in Chicago, but he probably won't go back there now that he knows me and Trav with you. I think he will be hard to find."

I gave her a disappointed look before turning to Trav. "You used to do security for this nigga. What you got?"

Trav turned the toothpick around in his mouth. "Carl is arrogant, but he smart. I agree with Kianna that finding him will be hard. I think we might have to bring him to us. Find a way to get him out in the open and then bust his shit."

"Also, I been watching the news," Fantasia cut in. "They saying the attack on Triple Time might've been a terrorist attack. Twenty-two people died and they calling it a mass shooting. That means the Feds is probably about to get involved. And I believe they might be watching Carl. If we go to Chicago and start shooting, that might not be good for us. I agree with Kianna and Trav. We have to bring him to us."

I took a moment to think about their advice. "Okay. I agree with y'all. So what we suggest? How y'all wanna hit 'em?"

"I say we keep it local," Damo jumped in. "Since we lost the plug, them TBT niggas been out there grinding. They think they own the streets. Let's start knocking they asses off and leave some calling cards. See if that bring him to us. And I know who we can hit first."

***

T-Rez wasn't hard to find. The local rapper's social media platforms were live and he was always posting about his next party or event. And it was no secret that T-Rez was TBT. He screamed it in every song and had it tattooed on his forearms. Trav found where he lived and Damo found us a way in. The key would be T-Rez's girlfriend's brother. He was sitting in the backseat of the Ford Escape between Damo as Fantasia. Me and Trav were up front. We sat outside the two-story brick house waiting for the opportunity to make our move. A small get together had just ended and everybody had gone home.

"Let's get it," I said, leading the way from the SUV.

Me and my killers wore black clothes, gloves, and face masks and carried silenced pistols. We walked up to the house with our special guest leading the way. When we were up on the porch, I put the gun to his head and stepped out of view. Trav rang the doorbell.

"Who is it?" T-Rez's girlfriend called from inside.

"It's Briant," the brother called.

Locks clicked and the door opened. I pushed the brother into the house and pointed my pistol in the woman's face.

"You bet' not scream, bitch!"

"Ahhhh!"

Clap!

The bullet went through her mouth and out the back of her head. Blood and brains sprayed as she fell to the floor.

"No!" Briant screamed.

Trav slapped him with the pistol as me and my niggas ran in the house. T-Rez was sitting on the couch playing a video game. When I shot his girlfriend, he lifted his hands and didn't move.

"T-Rez, what's good, my nigga?" I asked, walking over and waving my pistol.

"I don't got nothing in this house," the rapper squeaked, his eyes wide with fear.

"We didn't come for the goods, my nigga. We need information," Fantasia said.

"Tell us where Carl at," I said.

"He don't live in Milwaukee. He from Chicago."

"I know that. Tell me where he live."

"I never been to his house. I don't know."

I looked towards Damo. "Kill the brother."

Damo put his silenced pistol in the brother's face and squeezed the trigger twice. T-Rez closed his eyes and flinched like he got shot.

"Last chance, nigga. Tell me where Carl live. Tell me something, nigga."

"Okay. The nigga that's running shit name is Tone. He know more about Carl than anybody. Find him and he can tell you everything. His baby mama stay on 39th and Galena."

"Fuck Tone, nigga! Tell me where Carl live."

"That's all I know, my nigga. I don't know nothing else," he cried.

I believed him. So I turned to Trav. "He all yours."

Even though a mask was covering his face, I could see Trav's smile. He went to the kitchen and came back with a chair. After setting the chair in the middle of the room, he sat T-Rez in it and taped his arms and legs to the armrests and chair legs. Then he took off T-Rez's socks, balling them up and stuffing them in his mouth. He wrapped the tape around his head to keep the socks in his mouth.

"I learned this while living in Mexico," Trav said, pulling a straight razor from his pocket.

T-Rez began screaming as Trav shaved the Triple Beam Team tattoo from his forearm. Trav moved slowly, his hand steady as a surgeon's as he went to work cutting off the top layer of skin. The rapper had tattoos all over his body and Trav wanted to remove them all. After watching for a few minutes, I left with Damo. Trav and Fantasia stayed and had a party.

CHAPTER 10
Carl

I sat in the back of my bulletproof Range Rover, staring at the heap of burned bricks, mortar, and wood that used to be my club. Now Triple Time was a pile of ruins. A complete and total loss. Luckily I wasn't inside when Trav showed up with machine guns and bombs. Survivors said a rocket flew through the window and exploded near the bar. The people that ran outside died in a hail of bullets. There were whispers about Taliban, ISIS, or some kind of terrorist attack, but I knew the truth. The club had been blown up by my son. When Marie told me that Drayez was my seed, I went to find Kianna to stop her from killing him. When I got to the hotel, they were already gone. And now Kianna had betrayed me again. I wasn't going to give her a third strike.

"There go the boss," Billy said, pulling me from my thoughts.

I turned to look out the back window as the gray Rolls Royce truck pulled up behind the Range. I got out and walked to the rear passenger door. It opened, revealing the luxurious interior of the $200,000 SUV. Denzel Valentine waited inside.

"Cleaning up behind you is starting to get very expensive, Carl," he muttered. "The Feds are all over this and it's taking every resource that we have to keep you out of the spotlight and out of a cell."

"I shut them down in Milwaukee. I didn't think they would come here."

"I think your problem is that you don't think far enough ahead. I did some research, Carl, and found out Get Money Team is headed by a twenty-six-year-old boy. Drayez Alexander. A young punk that went to prison for stealing TVs out of Walmart. That's who you're getting beat by. A boy."

Several thoughts crossed my mind while he was talking. How the fuck did he find out about GMT so quickly? Did he know Drayez was my seed? Did he know about Kianna? And not far behind those questions was the thought of what Denzel would look like with a bullet in his forehead.

"The boy has a team, Denzel. You see what he did to my club. But I'm going to take care of it."

He gave an unimpressed snort. "You've been saying that for months. This is your final warning. Finish this nonsense. If I have to put out any more of your fires, your relationship with BBC will be terminated and you will be left to pick up the pieces on your own. Am I clear?"

I hated when he talked to me like I was a worker, but right now I needed his protection from the Feds.

"I'ma take care of it. You have my word."

He gave me a pitiful look. "There was a time when that used to mean something. You owe me, Carl. Get out of my truck."

I climbed from the Rolls, clenching my jaws so tight that it felt like my teeth were going to break. I hated Denzel's condescending tone and I hated even more that I needed his help. I climbed back in the Range, wishing I had a rocket launcher so I could blow Denzel's tolls Royce truck to smithereens.

"Where to, boss?" Billy asked.

"Just drive," I mumbled, pulling out my phone and calling Mikey Stokes.

"Carl, what's going on, brotha?"

"I just seen Denzel. I need to holla. Where you at?"

"Right now I'm getting my nails done at McNaily's on Michigan. Gimme about fifteen minutes and I can come to you."

"Stay where you at. I'm on the way," I said before ending the call. "Billy, go to the nail shop on Michigan."

During the drive to the nail shop, Tone called. I hoped he had good news.

"What's up, brah? Tell me something good."

"Man, Carl," he breathed. "It's all bad."

I closed my eyes and lay my head against the headrest. "C'mon, Tone. I can't take no more bad news. What happened?"

"It's T-Rez. They found him, his girl, and her brother a little while ago. All dead."

"Let me guess. Get Money team?"

"Yep. They tortured him, too. Shaved off all his tattoos and carved GMT into his chest."

I knew that was Trav's work. Sick-ass nigga was terrifying. "Okay. Tell everybody to keep they eyes open. Stay on point and be ready. We at war."

"I'm more than ready, Carl. I hope them niggas do come my way. I got some shit for they ass."

"Okay. I'ma be in this city in a little while. I'ma hit you later."

When we pulled up to these nail salon, I left Billy and Ren outside while I went inside. I found Mikey in a private room with a pretty young Asian woman doing his feet.

"Excuse us for a moment, Sue. I need to talk to my friend," he told the woman.

She got up and left quickly.

"What's up, Carl? What was the Godfather talking about?'

"Talking shit as usual. Said he will cut ties if I don't take care to this shit with GMT," I sulked, sitting in the chair across from him.

"I'ma be real with you, Carl. The shit you in is stretching our resources to the max. The shootout downtown and now the club. They saying it was terrorists. Feds all over this. Twenty-two people died. That's the worst mass killing Chicago's ever seen. You gotta figure out a way to end this shit with GMT, and then you gotta lay low for a long time. And you gotta start bringing in that money again. That's why he brought you in. I'm fighting for you to stay on the team, but you gotta help yourself."

"I appreciate the support. Good looking out. I'm trying to come up with a way to dead the shit, but the nigga got resources."

"How hard can it be to find and kill that nigga? Milwaukee is small. You gotta know somebody that know him. Six degrees of separation."

I let out a heavy sigh. "It's not that easy, my nigga. It's really, really complicated."

"No it's not." He chuckled. "We talking about millions of dollars. Real power. Plus, you haven't used BBC's resources yet. We have militias on standby. You've been using street niggas. Something like this takes pros."

I was silent for a moment, thinking. I wondered how he'd who react if he knew the truth.

"Drayez is my son."

Mikey looked like I just told him I bought a ticket to space. "Like blood? Fruit of yo' sack?"

I nodded.

He laughed. "Tell me you bullshitting, my nigga. Tell me you joking."

"And his partner is my ex. She helped me build TBT. They started GMT. I just found all of this shit out yesterday."

Mikey looked blown away. "Damn, Carl. What...the...fuck?"

"I told you it was complicated."

We sat in silence for a few moments.

"Damn, Carl. I'm sitting here trying to imagine the possibility of some shit like this happening. Gotta be one in a billion. Fuck that, one in a hundred billion. How the fuck did she meet him?"

"I don't know. I beat her ass and kicked her out about a year ago. Somehow they met. But I don't think she knows he my son, otherwise she wouldn't have fucked him. But that's not important. What's important is she used some of my old resources to turn him into a new me. Old dope connect. Old security. That's how he got the rocket launcher. Trav is ex-military and he's good."

Mikey shook his head. "That's crazy. So when did you find out he was your son?"

"A couple days ago. I used to fuck his mama back in the day. Before I did my bid. She ended up moving to Milwaukee. Turns out she was pregnant when she left. She heard I got life for murder so she didn't bother to reach out to me. Then we ran into each other at a gas station a little while ago and exchanged numbers. I get the call that he's my son right after I tried to kill him. That's why he blew up Triple Time."

Mikey shook his head again. "That sounds like a plot for a movie, my nigga."

"But this real life."

"I know," he nodded. "You familiar with the Bible?"

I gave him a questioning look. "What the Bible got to do with my situation?"

"Aaron and Moses. Moses was going to kill his son, Aaron, as a sacrifice to God to show him how deep his faith was. How serious is your faith in BBC?"

Me and Mikey held each other's stare for a moment. And then my phone rang. It was Tone. I knew it was more bad news.

"Yeah," I answered, letting out a heavy breath.

"The studio T-Rez was recording in just got hit. They saying it's on fire right now. I'm on my way over to check it out."

I locked eyes with Mikey. "Let me call you back, Tone."

"What happened? " Mikey asked.

I said one word. "Drayez."

"You say the word and I can round up my boys and send them to Milwaukee. You didn't raise him. You don't know him, and he probably don't even know that you his daddy. Your livelihood is at stake, Carl. Your freedom."

Even though I didn't know Drayez or raise him, the decision to kill him wasn't easy. He was my flesh and blood. The only real family I had left. My son. But he had taken so much from me. My brother. My club. Kianna. And now he was threatening to take BBC and my freedom. I knew what I had to do.

I searched my phone for Marie's number and made the call.

"Hey, Carl! What's up, nigga?"

"You know you got it, girl. I was just sitting here thinking about what we talked about the other day. I think I'm ready to meet Drayez. Did you tell him about me?"

"No. You told me you needed some time and I was respecting that."

"Good. I really appreciate that. Look, I'm on my way to the city in a couple of hours. Can I come by your house and talk to you before you introduce us?"

J-Blunt

CHAPTER 11
Drayez

I was back on my kill shit!

Carl still hadn't come to Milwaukee, so I was about to bring more heat. The next target was a nigga named Tone. T-Rez's info about Tone's baby mama was on point. Trav found her and did some recon. According to my head of security, Tone wasn't sweet. He kept a team of shooters with him at all times. But that didn't bother me none because the GMT hit squad was trained to go. There were seven of us on this move. Me, Damo, Trav, Fantasia, Bosco, Bryce, and Freeway. We were parked in different cars at opposite ends of the block. Me Trav, and Damo in one car, Bryce, Bosco, and Freeway in the other. Fantasia was trailing Tone and his niggas through the city. When Tone started heading our way, Fantasia would let us know and we would hit they asses from both directions.

While waiting for the call, I sat in the passenger seat, thinking about where I was going to relocate with my family. Me and Desiré talked about going west, California or Arizona. Los Angeles seemed like the place for me. Nice houses, beaches, and famous people. I could see us being the perfect family.

"I got the text," Trav said, cutting through my moment. "Fantasia said they coming up Galena. A black Maserati and a white Escalade. Four niggas in the car and five in the truck."

I gripped the AK-47 tightly, ready to bring the drama. "Text that to Bosco and tell him to follow our lead."

"Already on it, killa," Trav said as he sent the text.

I kept my eyes open, watching. Waiting. A few minutes later the Cadillac truck came into view. It drove past us followed by the Maserati. I waited until the vehicles parked.

"Let's get it!" I called, hopping out.

The Triple Beam Team niggas were laughing and talking loudly as they climbed from the truck and car. The first few of them didn't see us until it was too late.

Tat-tat-tat-tat-tat-tat! Tat-tat-tat-tat-tat-tat!

Bodies fell to the ground as me and my niggas fucked they worlds up. Some of the niggas tried to run and hide, but ended up running into Bosco n'em. The other niggas tried to get low in the vehicles, but we got on they asses too. I walked up to the Maserati and sprayed bullets until my chopper was empty. Trav and Damo fucked up the niggas in the Escalade. I turned to run back to the getaway car when Tone's baby mama's front door opened. A tall black-ass nigga with muscles like the Incredible Hulk stepped onto the porch holding a gun that looked like some shit out of a movie. It was about four feet long with six barrels. He seen us running away and took aim. The barrels began spinning and it sounded like thunder boomed as the gun started spitting fire.

"Get down!" Trav screamed.

Brrrreeeaaaaattt! Brrrreeeaaaaattt!

I dove onto the ground as everything around me was literally torn apart. Chunks of metal was ripped from the cars as glass shattered, and tires were flattened. I had never seen so much destruction happen so fast. Then it stopped. I poked my head up and seen the nigga turning the gun on my niggas. The barrels began spinning and thunder boomed as the weapon of destruction spat fire.

Brrrreeeaaaaattt! Brrrreeeaaaaattt!

My niggas didn't stand a chance. Bosco's body was literally torn in half, and Freeway's legs were blown off. Bryce made it to the car, but it didn't do him no good. The bullets tore the car into pieces and then it exploded. I stayed where I was and continued hiding. Wasn't no way I was fucking with that nigga.

When the shooting stopped, the Incredible Hulk nigga walked to the Escalade to check on his niggas. Trav jumped from his hiding spot and caught the nigga with his back turned.

Tat-tat-tat-tat-tat-tat!

When the nigga went down, I ran to the getaway car. What I seen had me stuck. Big-ass holes ripped through the car from the hood to the trunk.

"It ain't gon' start," Trav said, appearing at my side and telling me what I already knew.

"Here come Fantasia!" Damo said, pointing to the black Jeep speeding towards us.

"I heard the shooting. What happened?" Fantasia asked as we piled into the Jeep.

"Nigga had a Gatling gun!" Trav said in disbelief.

"What the fuck is a Gatling gun?" Damo asked.

"You just seen it," I answered, still a little shook up from this scene.

"Well, that should've got Carl's attention." Fantasia smiled.

***

We got away from Galena and were on our way to the auto salvage when I got a call from Marie.

"Now ain't a good time," I answered.

"I need to talk to you. Come by the house."

Something about the sound of her voice made the hairs on the back of my neck stand up. I could hear stress and fear. "What's up, Marie? You good?"

"Nah, I ain't good, boy. I told you that I need to talk to you."

"Now ain't a good time. What's going on?"

She got loud. "Drayez Alexander, get yo' black ass over here! I need to talk to you. It's an emergency."

"Okay. I'm on the way."

"And, Drayez," she said, her voice going soft. "I love you, son."

The phone hung up. I just stared at it. Marie just told me she loved me. I hadn't heard her say that since...shit, forever. Marie wasn't that emotional type. Something was wrong.

Damo noticed me staring at my phone. "You good, brah?"

"I don't know. That was Marie. She just told more she loved me."

"Something wrong with yo' mama saying she love you?" Fantasia asked.

"Yeah. Marie don't do that. Go by her house. She said it's an emergency. Load y'all clips."

I had moved Marie from 29th and Capitol to the suburbs in Waukesha. Mom's new neighborhood was quiet and filled with white homeowners. It was a little after 10:00 when Fantasia turned onto the block. Nothing looked out of the ordinary. Everything appeared normal.

"Somebody stay in the car and keep it running. One of y'all watch the block and one of y'all come with me," I said, grabbing a pistol and climbing from the truck.

"I'm coming with you," Fantasia said.

"I'ma watch the block. You stay in the truck, Damo," Trav said.

I tucked the pistol in my waist as Fantasia followed me up the walkway. Instead of barging into the house, I put my ear to the door to listen. I didn't hear anything crazy, so I used the key to let us in.

"Marie?" I called, pulling my pistol as we stepped into the living room.

Nobody answered.

"Marie, where you at?"

Still no answer.

Fantasia sniffed the air a couple of times, his eyes narrowing. "I smell blood," he whispered, pulling his pistol.

I did too. My heart sank to my feet as my worst nightmare played in my head.

We walked to the bedroom my mother shared with Keith. Found out where they smell of blood came from. Keith was on the floor, face down in a pool of blood. The back of his head was gone. Tears began to fill my eyes. Marie was dead, too. I could feel it.

We crept towards the kitchen, and that's where I found her. Marie was sitting in a chair, eyes closed, with blood covering her face and clothes and a bullet hole in her forehead. The sight made my heart explode and knees go weak.

"No, Momma!" I cried as I approached her.

I stood in front of her, numb with grief. There was a piece of paper in her lap. It said "BOOM". I picked it up and underneath it was a bomb. The red light glowed like the eye of the devil. And then it turned green.

Fantasia pushed me towards the window as the bomb exploded. I heard the boom and felt the heat as I flew out the window. I hit the ground and rolled across the lawn. I landed on my back, looking up at the stars. My ears rang and I could smell my burning skin. My entire body felt like it was on fire. And then everything went black.

J-Blunt

BOOK III: KARMA

KARMA - THE TOTALITY OF A PERSON'S ACTIONS DURING THEIR LIFE, WHICH DETERMINES THEIR FATE IN THE NEXT STAGE OF LIFE.

THE REPAYMENT OF DEEDS.

THE UNIVERSAL LAW OF SOWING AND REAPING.

KARMA IS BOTH GOOD AND BAD.

IF YOU DO GOOD, GOOD THINGS WILL HAPPEN TO YOU. IF YOU DO BAD, BAD THINGS WILL HAPPEN TO YOU.

EVERYONE IS CAPABLE OF DOING GOOD AND BAD - SOME WORSE THAN OTHERS.

THE POINT OF LIFE ISN'T HOPING THAT YOU NEVER DO A BAD THING OR RECEIVE BAD KARMA.

BUT INSTEAD, HOPE THAT YOUR GOOD DEEDS OUT-WEIGH THE BAD.

IF THEY DON'T, BEWARE, BECAUSE KARMA CAN BE A BITCH!

J-Blunt

CHAPTER 12
Carl

I didn't feel any remorse for the killings of my son and his mother. It had to be done. It was my life or his. Self-preservation is a must. Nobody's life was more important than mine. The law of the jungle is kill or be killed. I did what I had to do.

The phone rang, pulling me from my thoughts. It was Mikey.

"What's good, brotha?"

"Denzel wants to see you."

I blew out a frustrated breath. The last muthafucka on earth that I wanted to see was Denzel's bitch ass.

"What he want?"

"He didn't say. Wants you to meet him at Oliver's. You know where that is?"

"Yeah. Downtown. I'm leaving the house in a few minutes."

"How did that situation with your son go?"

I gave a small chuckle. "He had to go on a trip and I probably won't see him for a while."

"That sounds good. When I finish wrapping up my business, I'll catch up with you so we can talk in person."

"You got it, brah."

After ending the call with Mikey, I hopped in my bulletproof Range with my security and went to meet Denzel. When I walked in the restaurant, the maître d escorted me to Denzel's table in the back. He was sitting with a fine-ass woman that he quickly dismissed when I walked up. I locked eyes with her briefly as she walked away.

"Carl," Denzel nodded, looking me from head to toe.

"What's up, Denzel? Mikey said you wanted to talk."

He motioned towards the empty seat. "Have a seat. Pour yourself a drink."

I sat down and grabbed the bottle of red wine, filling my empty glass halfway.

"How is the situation in Milwaukee coming along?" he asked.

"I struck a major blow. The city should be ours now."

He lifted a brow. "Should be?"

"Is," I clarified. "The city is ours."

He eyed me over the rim of his glass of wine before taking a sip. "The house that got blown up in Milwaukee? That was you?"

I nodded. "That was his mother's house. I got her too."

Denzel looked impressed. "Well, let's make a toast to TBT taking over Milwaukee!"

I lifted my glass, tapping it against his.

"Now that you've taken care of that, I want you to move to Milwaukee to oversee the expansion of Triple Beam Team. We need to take over the entire city and all of GMT's enterprises."

I almost choked on my drink. "Move to Milwaukee?"

"That's right. We want the entire city. We cannot allow another clique to sprout up. GMT's demise means there will be an open market. You know the city, and I trust you to get things done."

"I don't shit in my backyard, Denzel. That's how come I haven't been knocked. TBT is in capable hands. The city is ours. Plus, I have property in Illinois. I can take care of things from here."

Denzel set the drink down and leaned forward, resting his elbows on the table, his stare serious. "I don't think you understand what I'm saying, Carl. I'm not asking you to move to Milwaukee. I'm telling you. I want that market. Plus, you need to leave Illinois for a while. The federal investigation into your club is heating up. I think it would easier to deal with if you were in Milwaukee. The downtown shooting and Triple Time being blown up has put a spotlight on you, and we don't need another incident to happen around you."

I mugged the shit out of Denzel's fake ass, wishing we were alone so I could pull the pistol from my waist and shoot him in the face. I hated him with a passion. And the fact that I had to follow his orders burned in my soul.

"Say no more, Denzel. I'ma make that move as soon as I can. Milwaukee will be ours."

He gave a smug smile. "I'm glad we can easily agree. Cooperation goes long way in this organization, Carl. A long way."

Instead of slapping the nigga's mustache off like I wanted to do, I nodded. "I hear you, brotha. If we done, I'ma get outta here and get started on the move."

Denzel lifted his glass in a toast. "Good luck."

I walked away from the table barely able to keep my cool. This bitch-ass nigga just forced me to move to Milwaukee and I didn't have a choice but to move. I felt like a worker and hated every moment of it.

As I was walking towards the front door, I spotted the woman that I replaced at Denzel's table leaving the bathroom, also heading for the exit. We locked eyes for a moment, and that's when I got a thought. I needed to see who she was. If she was Denzel's bitch, I was going to try to fuck her. She was a well of information and I needed that to get Denzel's bitch ass.

"Let me get the door for you." I smiled, putting my chivalry on full display while I checked out her goods.

She was average height with long permed hair and a pretty face. She wore a form-fitting cream dress that fit just right. And her body was nice and tight. Nothing too big. Everything just right for her frame.

"Thank you." She smiled. "You are a gentleman."

"You're welcome. That dress looks like it was made for you. A-plus to your stylist."

She gave a smirk while smiling at me with her eyes. "It was made for me. One of a kind. I designed it and I'm my own stylist."

I gave a nod. "I'm impressed. You killed it," I complimented while following her to the valet station. "Do you have a card, in case I need some work done?"

She gave a warning look. "Be careful, Carl."

I laughed. "My intentions are pure, Miss…?"

"Cantrell. I'm Denzel's girlfriend," she answered, handing the valet her ticket.

"How long have you had that problem?" I cracked.

She laughed. "Five years."

"Girlfriend, huh? Why not wife?"

She studied my face for a moment. "Why are you so nosy?"

"It's human nature to be curious. Plus, Denzel doesn't deserve you. It shouldn't take a man five years to find out if he wants to spend the rest of his life with you."

Cantrell looked away. I had touched a nerve.

"Some things just aren't meant to be."

"That's not true. We make our own reality. We are the masters of our fate. This captains of our souls. We control our destiny. If you leave your happiness or fate up to anything or anyone outside of you, nothing will ever be meant to be. You'll always be waiting."

Me and Cantrell shared a long stare. My words were having an effect. Then the valet pulled up in a white Lexus and Ren pulled up in the Range Rover.

"This is my ride, Carl. It was nice to meet you."

"Wait. I need to know how to reach you in case I need some custom work."

She smiled at me before getting in the car and driving away.

"What was that about?" Ren asked when I climbed into the truck.

Ren and Billy had been sent by Denzel, so I had to be careful what I said around them.

"Cantrell. She a fashion designer. But she is the least of our worries. Denzel want me to move to Milwaukee ASAP. Y'all coming with me."

Billy looked over the passenger seat. "As long as I got money and pussy, it don't matter where we go."

I went home to pack and make arrangements to find a house in Milwaukee. Mikey showed up a few hours later.

"I heard about the move. Sorry I couldn't give you a heads up. I didn't know."

"Don't trip, brah. Nothing you could have done about it anyway."

"You're taking it better than expected. I thought you would be snapping out."

"Getting mad won't change nothing. Plus, I think Denzel wanted me to get mad. I seen it in his eyes. So I'ma do one better and get even. You ready to make that move? You ready to be on top?"

Mikey shifted uncomfortably. "You still on that?"

"C'mon, brah. Don't back out on me now. That's yo' spot and I'ma help you get it."

"How will you help me be the leader of BBC? Denzel is powerful. People look up to him and respect him. If something happens to him, I don't want my name connected to it."

"And it won't. I think I discovered the key to his downfall. Who is Cantrell?"

Surprise spread across Mikey's face. "How did you find out about Cantrell?"

"I seen her when I met Denzel. We had a conversation while waiting on the valet to bring her car. Who is she? What is she about? Is she loyal?"

Mikey looked away and shook his head. "Cantrell is like a mythical creature. I don't know shit about her. I knew this nigga since we were teenagers and I probably only heard him talk about her a hand full of times. And I only had a couple conversations with her. She don't talk around me."

The news surprised me. Why wouldn't Denzel's right hand and day one know anything about his main thang?

"You think he hiding her?"

"To be honest, I don't know. Denzel is one or those serious niggas that don't play around or bullshit. Been like that forever. He wasn't the type of nigga that slayed a bunch of bitches. He keep the one he with."

I stored what he said in the back of my mind. "That's good to know. I believe Cantrell is the way to get this nigga. She knows shit about him that you don't know. The intimate shit. His secrets. We need those secrets to bring him down, and I'ma get 'em."

***

One week later

It didn't take long to get my TBT niggas focused on our mission to take over all of GMT's action. After doing a little digging, I found out that GMT operations ceased right after Diego got knocked. And now that Drayez was dead, the clique was in shambles. The ones with no guidance or drive were left to starve. A few of them even joined our side during the Triple Beam Team takeover. And since the takeover was going so smoothly, I had a little extra time on my hands. I used it to track down Cantrell. She owned a boutique clothing store called Exquisite on the west side to Chicago.

"You want me to come in with you?" Ren asked.

"This a one man job. I'ma be right back," I said as I climbed from the Range.

I strolled through the glass double doors of the boutique and took a look around. It was a small woman's store, so I got a few questioning looks from the women shoppers. I ignored them and let my eyes roam around the store until I found Cantrell. She was near the back helping a customer and didn't see me walk in.

"Can I help you, sir?" a pretty young dark-skinned woman asked.

"No, thanks. I'm just looking," I said before walking away.

I tried to be inconspicuous as I searched the racks of clothing while making my way towards the back of the store. When I was a few feet away from Cantrell, I bumped into a rack, spilling clothes on the floor. That got her attention.

"Oh shit! Sorry about that," I apologized, bending to pick up the garments.

"Excuse me, Sheryl," Cantrell said before coming to help me. "What are you doing here, Carl?" she asked, not bothering to hide her irritation.

"Is that how you greet all your customers?"

"No. Just the ones that come into my store and knock all my clothes on the floor."

"It was an accident." I chuckled while hanging the last piece of clothing back on the rack.

"I don't believe you. And how did you find me?"

100

"When a man wants something, there are no such thing as obstacles."

She tried to keep a serious face but lost the battle and smiled. "You're making a mistake, Carl. I'm already taken."

"Your body is taken, but your mind and heart are free."

She shook her head. "I think you should leave before you get in trouble."

I stepped close, invading her space. "What if I like trouble?"

She took a step back. "You don't want my problems, Carl. Trust me. I'm not who you think I am. I'm not worth you getting into trouble with Denzel."

I stepped close to her again. "You let me worry about trouble. I can take care of myself. And I can take care of you, too. Better than Denzel. He doesn't deserve to be with you if he can't commit to you. I know your worth. I see you."

She took another step back. "Please, Carl. Don't do this. I think you're a nice guy, but I'm not going there with you. I'm not that kind of girl. My workers are starting to get nosy and I don't want to be the topic of any gossip. I need you to leave. Please."|

I looked around and seen that we had become the center of attention for a few of her employees. It was time to go.

"Okay, Cantrell. I don't want you to get in trouble, so I'll leave. But answer me one question. You said you're not who I think you are. What does that mean? Who are you?"

She looked away. "I already said too much. I really need you to leave."

I began walking backwards towards the door. "I guess I'll see you next lifetime."

J-Blunt

CHAPTER 13
Six months later

It felt like I was having a déjà vu moment.

I was sitting in the office at my new club, CC's, short for Cartier Chris, when I had the déjà vu moment. It felt like I was sitting in Triple Time again getting ready for its grand opening. As I sat in the plush leather chair, getting lost in the reverie, I remembered how excited Chris was for this club to open. Kianna was standing by my side being a loving and supporting woman. The night was filled with ups and downs. When I got caught getting my dick sucked behind the bar, Kianna went crazy.

Kianna?

Where the fuck was she? I had been in Milwaukee for six months and she hadn't showed herself. Was she mad at me for having Drayez and his mother killed? What did she expect? That nigga was my enemy. Was she my enemy, too? I told her to kill him and she didn't do it. She chose her side. She was GMT. And the next time I seen her, I was going to treat her like an op. Then there was Trav. I had watched Fantasia go in the house with Drayez before it blew up. I knew Trav wasn't going to let me get away with killing his little brother. He was going to hit back. And I was prepared.

A light knock on the door interrupted my thoughts. When it opened, Sheila walked in looking like she stepped out of a fantasy. Hair in long curls hanging past her shoulders, perfectly done makeup, and the Valentino dress hugged her in all these right places, showing off her perfect body.

"Hey, baby. Are you ready for the big opening?"

"Hell yeah!" I grinned. "I was just thinking about when I opened Triple Time in Chicago. It feels like déjà vu. I want it to be a success."

She walked around the desk to kiss me on the lips. "It will be a success, baby. There is a long line of people standing outside waiting to get in. Young Ced is performing. We're buzzing all over social media. Tonight's going to be lit, baby."

"I know. And having you as the host wearing this dress is going to drive everyone crazy. You killing it, baby," I complimented, giving her ass an affectionate slap.

The front doors to CC's officially opened at 8:00 and the people began pouring in. I had eye candy behind the bar pouring drinks, more eye candy in my bottles girls, and Sheila's fine ass was the host. I mingled with the crowd, encouraged the bad bitches to be bad, and the ballers to ball. The night was going perfect until Denzel's bitch ass walked in. He was followed by Mikey, Cantrell, and their security. I had Sheila find them a spot in VIP while I went to greet them.

"Denzel! Mikey! I wasn't expecting to see y'all!" I greeted the men, purposely leaving Cantrell out.

"I wouldn't miss this for nothing in the world," Denzel smiled, shaking my hand as he looked around. "The place looks really nice."

"Hey, Carl," Mikey said dryly.

I took note of his sour mood and planned to find the cause of it later. Then I turned my attention to Cantrell.

"And who do we have here?"

Denzel looked to his woman briefly. "This is Cantrell. Do you have somewhere for us to sit?"

"VIP!" I smiled before leading the way. After they were seated, I waved a bottle girl over. "What are y'all drinking? How many bottles?"

"Since it's a celebration, bring us a bottle of champagne," Denzel said.

I looked to Mikey. "Just one? You don't want anything?"

"We're not staying long."

"We just wanted to come show our support for you," Denzel chimed in. "TBT's success means BBC's success."

"I can drink to that," I said before turning to the bottle girl. "Bring us a bottle of Ace and four glasses."

She returned with a bottle on ice and four glasses. I poured everyone drinks and lifted my glass for a toast.

"To long life, success, and black billionaires!"

After clinking glasses, we all took drinks.

"There you are, Carl. I've been looking for you," Sheila said, popping up on my side.

"Hey, baby. What's up?"

"I need to steal you away real quick."

When I looked towards Denzel, he was eyeing Sheila. I decided to introduce her to everyone.

"Denzel, Mikey, this is my backbone, Sheila. Sheila, these are my partners, Denzel and Mikey. And she's Cantrell," I added lastly, loving the anger and envy that flashed in Cantrell's eyes.

"Hi everybody!" Sheila waved.

Denzel and Mikey nodded. Cantrell snarled.

"Excuse me for a moment," I said before walking away with Sheila. "What's up, baby?"

Her face turned serious. "Young Ced's security is tripping. You need to handle it."

I walked to the back of the club and seen Young Ced's entourage surrounded by my security. Since I had moved to Milwaukee, I tripled my security detail and kept at least ten hitters around me. And these weren't street niggas with quick trigger fingers, but professionals. Niggas that had been trained by the military and had done tours in the war zones of Iraq and Afghanistan.

"What's going on?" I asked, announcing my presence.

"You need to check yo' niggas before they get what they really don't want!" Young Ced mouthed.

He was a little nigga, 5'5" and 100 pounds soaking wet. The short, colorful dreadlocks and tattoos all over his face and body made him look like every young nigga that I passed in the street. And his entourage was small. Him and five niggas that looked like they all grew up in the same hood. Instead of giving the little nigga's words some attention, I turned to my head of security.

"What's going on, Billy?"

"These niggas disrespectful. I told them to give up they guns and they started talking shit."

I turned back to Young Ced. "Don't nobody bring heat in here except us. My house, my rules. My security is well-trained. These niggas been in real combat. Now, I want to give you this $25,000 that I set aside and I want you to entertain my guests. But if you can't go by my rules, you and yo' niggas can leave and I'll keep my money."

Young Ced looked to someone in his entourage. A tall stocky nigga wearing Cartier glasses gave the young rapper a nod. Ced turned back to me. "A'ight, family. But if somethin' pop off, them niggas betta be ready."

"We stay ready so we won't have to get ready," I quipped.

After dealing with the rapper, I headed back towards the front of the club. I was walking to the bar when someone caught my eye. She was sexy, cute, and fine, all at the same time. Peanut butter complexion, long hair that fell past her shoulders, round face with pretty brown eyes, and a pair of juicy lips that looked like she could suck the skin off a nigga's dick. Her body was unbelievable. She was tall and thick like Megan Thee Stallion. The skintight gold bodysuit that she wore showed every curve. Big titties that looked like they wanted to pop out of the top. Small waist. Wide hips. Ass so big that you could see it from the front. When we made eye contact, she looked me from head to toe and smiled. I was definitely fucking her tonight!

"Carl?"

I turned and seen two niggas approaching from my right. One tall and slinky. The other short with a wide body. I didn't know them, but since they were guests on opening night, I decided to entertain them.

"What's going on, fellas? Everything good?"

"We was wondering if we could holla at you," the tall one said.

I glanced from the niggas towards the Megan Thee Stallion lookalike only to see that she had disappeared. Damn!

"What y'all got? Make it quick 'cause I'm busy," I said, looking around for the vixen.

"We wanna join the team."

That got all of my attention. I looked the niggas over, judging their worth. "Who the fuck is y'all and what team is y'all talking about joining?"

"I'm Blaze and this my nigga, Hood." the shorter one introduced. "We wanna get in with Triple Beam Team. We used to be GMT, but y'all got the city on lock and we wanna eat."

I studied the niggas' faces to see what they were up to. Some kind of hidden agenda. Treachery. But the only thing I could see was the gleam. These niggas was starving and wanted to eat. But I wasn't going to make it that easy.

"Why should I let y'all niggas have a seat at my table? Y'all was with my enemy. Y'all probably killed some of my niggas. Y'all think I'm supposed to open the door and let y'all in?"

"We not down with that beef shit. We just wanna eat," Blaze said.

"And whatever we gotta do to eat with you, we gon' do it," Hood added.

I studied them for a moment, making them squirm. "Where is Kianna and Trav?"

They looked to each other before shrugging their shoulders.

"Ain't nobody seen 'em since Drayez got blew up," Blaze said.

"Once we found about Drayez getting killed, we knew GMT was over and everybody went they separate ways," Hood added.

"Well, I guess this conversation is over. If y'all don't got nothing for me, I don't got nothing for y'all," I said before turning away.

"Hold on, Carl!" Hood called.

I spun back around. "What up?"

"If we find them, can we eat with you?"

"It'll be a buffet, my nigga. All you can eat." I grinned before walking away.

I looked around for the thick woman again and spotted Cantrell heading towards the bathroom. We locked eyes for a moment and she mugged me before closing the door. I couldn't help but smile, loving the game. I loved it so much that I went into the woman's bathroom and locked the door behind me. There were three stalls. Two of them were empty. I leaned against the wall and waited silently. The toilet flushed and a few moments later, Cantrell walked out of the stall.

"What are you doing in here, Carl?" she asked, cutting her eyes at me as she headed for the sink.

"I wanted to see you again. To talk."

She met my eyes in the mirror while washing her hands. "Why do you want to see me? You already have a 'backbone'. What would she think if she found you in here talking to me?"

"I don't want to talk about Sheila. We need to be talking about why Denzel introduced you as Cantrell. Why not his woman or backbone?"

"My relationship with Denzel is fine. We don't need titles," she said, unable to hide the lie in her eyes.

I walked up behind her, pressing my dick against her ass, my hands on her shoulders. "You can't hide the truth. Your eyes betray you," I whispered in her ear.

"Why can't you leave me alone?" she protested weakly.

"Because Denzel doesn't deserve you. You deserve to be with me," I said, letting my hands slide down her shoulders, caressing her breasts. I moved down to her ass and tried to reach under her dress, but she grabbed my hand in a tight grip

"No!" she said forcefully. "We have to stop before this goes too far. I'm not who you think I am."

I studied her face in the mirror, trying to read between the lines. What was she trying to tell me?

A knock on the door interrupted our moment.

"Hey! Open the door! I gotta pee!" a woman called from the hallway.

"To be continued." I smiled before unlocking the door and walking out.

I headed back to the club, stopping to take a look around. CC's was packed and everybody looked like they were having a good time. My night was going good. And when I spotted Mikey by the bar, I knew the night was going to get better.

"What's up, partner?" I asked, clasping a hand on his shoulder as I sat on the stool next to him.

"Hey, Carl," he said dryly before downing a shot.

"It's been that kind of night, huh?"

He let out a frustrated breath. "Being around this high fallutingass nigga is starting to be too much. Nigga act like he my daddy or something. BBC wouldn't be shit without me. I'm the one doing all the work. All he do is sit back and tell muthafuckas what to do. He don't do no work. I do everything, but he try to treats me like a peon. I'm tired of that shit."

I smiled on the inside, but kept my face serious. "You should be the one in charge, Mikey. I think the person doing all the work should be calling to shots."

"I know. I love that nigga like a brother, but I'm tired of being treated like a flunky. We supposed to be equal. That's how it started. We was partners. Then he got big-headed."

"Ain't no since remaining loyal to a nigga that ain't loyal to you. You gotta step out from behind that nigga's shadow. It's your time, Mikey. This is your opportunity. You ready?"

He looked at me and I could see the lack of confidence in his eyes.

"I don't know, Carl."

I leaned in close. "I know it's your time, Mikey. You can do this. You said it yourself; you do more than Denzel. Now you don't gotta do it for him no more. You can do it for yourself. If you say the word, I'll take care of the rest. Just say the word. You ready?"

We had a staring contest.

"Okay. I'm ready."

I no longer hid my smile. "Give me the all information you have on his head of security and I'll handle the rest."

J-Blunt

CHAPTER 14

The rest of the night went by in a breeze. Young Ced put on a show that had the club shaking. When he performed "Twerk Something", the women went crazy and an ass shaking contest popped off, the winner getting $2,500.

The lights came on at 2:00 and it was time to clean up and count the profits. I didn't leave until about 3:30. My security led the way out the back door, checking the alley before giving the all clear.

I had just stepped into the parking lot when an engine revved. I looked up as headlights came on and a car sped towards us. My security sprang into action, pulling their weapons and fanning the car with bullets. The bullet-riddled car crashed into the side of the building. My security kept their guns drawn as they surrounded the car. Whoever was in the car had to be dead.

"Ain't nobody in here," Ren announced after checking the car.

A cold feeling entered my bones. "What you mean ain't nobody in the car?"

He poked his head in the car to look around. "It's rigged to drive itself. Ain't nobody in here."

A bright light behind us got our attention. I turned my head just in time to see fire sparking from the barrel of a machine gun.

"It's a fifty! Get down!" someone screamed.

Billy dove on top of me as the loudest gun I ever heard tore up everything around me. I could hear my security screaming as .50 caliber bullets tore them apart. The gunfire lasted about thirty seconds before a black Jeep sped away. I stood to my feet, looking around in awe. Everything around us had bullet holes in it. Not even my bulletproof Range Rover could withstand the machine gun bullets. The windows were shattered and holes as big as baseballs were in the body. Three members of my security also lay on the ground. One was missing an arm. Another one was missing his head.

"Did anybody see who was driving the Jeep?" Billy asked.

Everybody shook their heads, confusion on their faces. Even though I didn't see his face, I knew who was driving the Jeep. And whenever the opportunity presented itself, I was going to fuck him up.

***

A couple days later I was back in my club, trying to process everything that happened opening night. Three of my niggas were killed and there was a lot of damage to my building from the armor piercing .50 caliber rounds. I knew, without a shadow of a doubt, that Trav was behind the attack. To get a .50 caliber machine gun, you needed connections. To get armor piercing rounds was damn near impossible. The only nigga that I knew capable of getting that type of weapon and artillery was Trav. My club opening was all over social media and he showed up to ruin it with my murder. Since he missed, he would come at me again. And I would be ready.

My cell phone buzzing pulled me from my thoughts. It was Billy.

"Yeah?"

"I got two niggas outside. Hood and Blaze. You know these niggas?"

I thought back to the ex-GMT niggas I met during the grand opening. "Yeah. Send them in. You come, too. I think these niggas might have something that we need."

A few moments later, the two starving hustlers walked in my office followed by Billy.

"Blaze! Hood! What's good?" I asked.

"What's up, Carl?" Blaze smiled, giving me a nod.

"Y'all relax. Have a seat. Y'all here because y'all got something for me, right?"

"We heard about what happened after the club closed the other night," Hood said. "Niggas been talking about it all over the city."

"What they saying?" I asked.

"That it was Trav," Blaze confirmed.

"And y'all here because y'all finna tell me where he is, right?"

The niggas shared a look before Hood spoke up. "We don't know where he live, but we know where he gon' be tonight."

"Him and Kianna," Blaze added.

That got my attention. "What about Kianna? Where she at?"

"We don't know where she at right now, but she supposed to be with Trav tonight. She his woman now, I think."

I laughed and shook my head. Trav finally got her.

"So, where will they be tonight? I'm dying to know."

"They supposed to be meeting at Washington Park tonight around 10:00. They meeting with some other GMT niggas to try and bring the clique back together."

I shot Billy a quick glance. He gave a quite nod.

"That sounds real good, my niggas. If everything check out, we gon' get a lot of money together. In the meantime, let me show y'all what y'all can look forward to. Show y'all how TBT fuck it up."

I led Blaze and Hood through the club, pausing to alert my security and to grab some women and drinks. We left the club in my new bulletproof Cadillac Escalade, courtesy of Denzel. After the attack by Trav, he sent me another bulletproof SUV. Once I was in the armored truck with the potential TBT members and the women, we drove around smoking and drinking. Fifteen minutes later, Billy parked in front of the house my nigga Donovan was killed in.

"Ladies, hang out in the truck. We'll be right back. Hood and Blaze, come with me. I need to show y'all something."

I hopped out of the Lac truck followed by the ex-GMT niggas, Billy, and Ren. I left two cars of security outside to watch my back. When we were in the house, I got right down to business, pulling the .45 Desert Eagle from my waist and pointing it in Blaze's face.

"Tell me where the fuck Trav at or I'ma blow yo' nose off, bitch!"

"C'mon, brah! Chill! We ain't on that!" he panicked, throwing his hands in the air.

I slapped him in the face with the cannon, knocking him to the ground. Then I turned to Hood. "I ain't playing, nigga! If y'all muthafuckas don't tell me where Trav at, I'ma cut y'all assess up and feed y'all to some dogs."

"I don't know where he at, my nigga. On my mama I don't!" Hood swore.

I slapped him in the face with the pistol too, dropping him next to his nigga.

"You muthafuckas think I'm stupid, huh? I know y'all li'l bitch asses spied on me so Trav could make the hit later that night. But that bitch-ass nigga missed. And y'all stupid asses was dumb enough to come back to the scene. One of y'all better say something before I start letting this bitch ride."

"I don't know nothing, my nigga. We just wanna eat," Blaze cried, holding his jaw.

I looked to Billy and Ren. "Stomp they asses."

My security went to work on Blaze first. They kicked and stomped his ass good, making him call out to God and his mother. Then they did the same thing to Hood. When they were done, both combat trained men were breathing hard like they had run a race. Hood and Blaze were bleeding and groaning in agony.

"Somebody better tell me something, because it's only gon' get worse. Where the fuck is Trav?"

"I don't know, Carl. Please let us go. We wasn't tryna set you up," Blaze pleaded.

I studied the wounded men for a moment, wondering if they were telling the truth. I still wasn't convinced, so I went to the kitchen and grabbed a big-ass butcher knife. I kneeled next to Blaze and pointed the knife in his face.

"This yo' last opportunity. Where the fuck is Trav?"

He looked at the knife, terror lighting his eyes. "I-I don't know, fam."

I lifted the knife over my head and drove it through his eye with all my strength. Half the knife disappeared into his eye socket, getting stuck. Blaze screamed and began thrashing around on the floor. I took a few steps back and watched him jerk around for a few moments. Then he stopped moving.

I pointed my pistol at Hood. "Where the fuck is Trav?"

"Okay, brah! I'ma tell you everything. Please don't kill me," he begged, the fear of God in his eyes.

I put my pistol away. "Okay, I won't kill you. Tell me everything."

"Trav did send us to spy on you. He sent us again to set you up. He waiting for you at Washington Park."

I stared at him for a moment, picturing how he would look with the knife in his eye. "Is Kianna with him?"

"Yeah. She his bitch now. She in on the set-up."

Hearing the words felt like a stab to the heart. She betrayed me for the third time. There wouldn't be a fourth.

"A'ight, li'l nigga. I'ma keep my word. I'm not going to kill you."

Relief washed over his face.

I looked to Billy. "Kill him."

***

I spent the rest of the day going over the plan to kill Trav with my team. Trav expected me to show up with my niggas and come in hard. Then he would hop out and kill us. He would probably use a bomb or the .50 again. Maybe he had a clique of killers waiting to ambush. I had to be ready for any and everything. Trav was a trained killer and not to be taken lightly.

When it was time to move out, my team piled into five SUVs. Two of them were filled with the decoys, loyal TBT soldiers that would do anything for the team. Of course, they didn't know about the trap they were walking into. I was using them as bait, sending them into the bear trap and hoping the bear would expose himself. When we got to the park, the decoy SUVs drove ahead while the other three set up in strategic positions around the park. When everyone was set, I radioed the decoys to go ahead. I watched through night vision binoculars as the ten untrained men piled out of the trucks and walked brazenly through the park with their guns out.

Billy shook his head. "They all about to die."

"The pawn's job is to protect the king," I said.

"That's cold." Ren chuckled.

"Bundle up."

Silence filled the truck as we watched, waiting for the action.

"We move as soon as the fireworks start," Ren reminded.

We didn't have to wait long. There was a small flash from a wooded area right before an explosion lit up the night. It looked like a bomb detonated in the middle of the decoys. Most of them went down.

"The show started! Let's move!" Billy yelled, grabbing his assault rifle and jumping from this truck.

"Everybody go! " I radioed, grabbing the .45 caliber Israeli Uzi and following Billy. While running towards the action, I held the binoculars in place and watched my sacrificial lambs get slaughtered. After the explosion, three figures dressed in black came out on the water in the lagoon firing automatic rifles. My lambs didn't stand a chance.

"Three came from the water and there is one hiding in the trees with explosives!" my radio chirped.

We were about 200 yards from the shooters when they noticed us. Then all hell broke loose. They turned their guns on us, forcing me to hit the ground as bullets whizzed by. There were several flashes from the wooded area and I knew what was to follow. I put my face in the dirt, plugged my ears, closed my eyes and hoped I didn't get blown to pieces.

Kaboom! Kaboom! Kaboom!

I could feel the earth shake around me as several explosions lit up the night. When everything stopped vibrating, I opened my eyes and looked around. Several of my niggas got caught in the blast. Billy's body was twisted at an awkward angle and he was missing an arm. Gunfire and muzzle flashes continued to light up the night as the rest to my team arrived to engaged Trav and his niggas. A few moments later, the gunfire stopped. I hit the key on my radio.

"I need a report. Somebody give me a report!"

"All enemies are deceased. All enemies are deceased," my radio cracked.

Relief flooded my body as I got up from the ground.

"Find Trav," I radioed. "I need to see a body."

We went to check the bodies near the lagoon first. Three niggas dressed in black lay near the water dead.

"Pull the masks up so I can see."

A quick inspection showed than none of them were Trav. I got a sinking feeling in my gut.

"We got one alive near the woods," my radio squawked.

I jogged over to where my team had the body surrounded with their guns drawn.

"Take off his mask," I ordered.

One of my security bent down to remove the mask. It was Trav. He was wounded badly, bleeding from the chest.

"Damn, Trav. Looks like you fucked up. Turns out yo' ass ain't bulletproof," I cracked.

He let out a painful laugh, blood dripping from his mouth. "Fuck you, Carl. You still a bitch-ass nigga."

I lifted the Uzi to his face. "Where is Kianna, nigga?"

He choked up another laugh. "Now I see why you want her back so bad. That pussy fiya!"

I stomped him in the chest. "You think this shit funny, bitch-ass nigga? Where the fuck is Kianna?"

Sirens in the distance got our attention.

"We gotta go," Ren warned.

I moved my gun closer to Trav's face. "Last chance, nigga. Where is Kianna?"

Trav let out another painful laugh.

I was about to squeeze the trigger when Trav's hand caught my eye. There was a grenade in his hand and his thumb had just removed the pin. My instincts took over and I grabbed the person nearest me. It was Ren. I didn't have time to consider what I was doing because I was in survival mode. I threw Ren on top of Trav and took off running.

"Grenade!" someone yelled.

I took about five steps before the grenade blew up. Because of my quick thinking, the grenade didn't have a big blast. I ran to my truck knowing that Ren's sacrifice saved my life.

J-Blunt

CHAPTER 15

Knowing that I killed two of my worst enemies had me in a perpetually good mood. Drayez was dead. Trav was dead. The final kill on my quest for revenge was Kianna, and I wouldn't rest until I put a bullet in her head.

When the weekend came, the club was back in full swing. Even though Trav had fucked up the end of my grand opening last weekend, the show went on. For the second weekend in a row I hired entertainment. 50Cal was performing on the stage and the crowd went crazy. I watched from the VIP, surrounded by security, enjoying the party vibe. And that's when I seen her. It was the thick and fine woman that got away last weekend. She stood in the middle of the crowd, giving me strong eye contact. Through the distance, I could see what her eyes were saying. She wanted me. This time, she wasn't going to get away.

"I'll be right back," I told Sheila as I got up from the table.

I maintained eye contact with the sexy stranger while closing the distance. She wore a tight black dress that barely covered her thighs, and the plunging neckline had her cleavage on full display. She was bouncing to the music, her wide hips swaying back and forth. I walked up on her, attempting to whisper in her ear.

"Hold on, man! What you doing?" she yelled, pushing me away and looking me up and down.

I lifted my hands. "I was trying to whisper in your ear so I wouldn't have to scream."

She turned her defense down a little. "Oh. You gotta say something, man. I didn't know what you was on. It's a lot of crazy people out here."

"I get it. My name is Carl. You wanna come kick it in VIP?"

She looked towards the VIP section and shook her head. "I'm good. I wanna stay on the floor and dance. You can dance, right?"

I did a two-step. "You ain't know!"

She laughed. "Hi, Carl. I'm Tracy."

"Okay, Tracy. Let me see what you got," I said, clearing a little room for her to dance.

"I'ma show you how to do a real two step. Yours was a little stiff," she teased before doing a sexy two step, twirling and poking her ass out a little. "Now what you got?"

I rolled my shoulders and popped the kinks out of my neck. "Back in the day we called this the wop," I said before busting a move.

"C'mon, Carl. You dancing like an old man. Look like you doing the Carlton dance." Tracy laughed. "Here goes something you should be able to do. The Toosie Slide."

I watched as she did the dance challenge made famous by Drake.

"I gotta be honest, Tracy. I don't know much about dancing and I don't wanna make a bigger fool of myself than I already have. I was just tryna be a good sport," I admitted.

"What's going on, baby?" Sheila asked, appearing at my side.

"Tracy was just showing me that I can't dance." I laughed.

The women did a quick inspection of one another.

A sparkle shone in Tracy's eyes as she sucked her teeth and licked her lips. Then she extended a hand. "You are so beautiful, Sheila. I'm Tracy."

"Thank you," Sheila blushed. "You are beautiful, too. Sorry that Carl can't dance, but maybe I can take his place."

Tracy looked Sheila over one more time. "I would love to dance with you."

"Oh, it's like that?" I laughed, feeling left out.

"Yep!" Sheila sang, reaching for Tracy's hand.

"Just like that!" Tracy added as the women ignored me and began dancing.

I went back to the VIP and watched the women dance. They started off innocent, laughing and playing. When 50Cal started performing his strip club anthem, "Do It for a Real Nigga", the ladies turned up. They began grinding, twerking, and slapping ass. After having their fun on the dance floor, they joined me in the VIP, sitting on my lap, one on each leg.

"I thought you was too good for the VIP section," I teased Tracy, loving the feel of her big soft ass on my lap.

"If I would've known Sheila was here, I would've been joined the party," she said, staring at my girl with lust in her eyes.

"And we want to continue the party in private," Sheila said, leaning forward and giving me a sexy kiss.

"We can't leave right——" I was saying when Tracy's mouth found mine.

She kissed me aggressively, forcing her tongue in my mouth and grabbing my dick through my pants. When Sheila joined in, we shared a sloppy three-way kiss.

"I want her now," Tracy said after we came up for air.

"Fuck it. Let's go to my office."

While I locked the door, the women kissed and groped their way over to the couch. I took off my suit jacket and went to join them.

"No," Tracy stopped me, putting a hand on my chest. "Just watch."

I moved her hand, looking at her like she was crazy. "Yeah, right. Stop bullshitting."

"I'm not playing. I don't sleep with men on the first night."

We had a stare-off. She was serious.

"Oh, you for real?"

"Yes." She smiled pecking me on the lips. "Have a seat and watch the show. Next time it'll be your turn."

I didn't know if I should be mad or not. A part of me felt like she was adding some spice to the situation by forcing me to watch. The other part of me was mad that I couldn't join in. I was horny as a muthafucka and I wanted to fuck her from the back so bad. But wanting to be a good sport, I went with the flow and sat down at my desk. They weren't going to leave me out. They couldn't.

The women took off their dresses, neither one wearing undergarments. Sheila's beautifully proportioned body looked amazing. Perfectly shaped perky titties that I loved sucking. Flat stomach. Small waist. Meaty and bald pussy. Tracy carried more weight than Sheila, but it was in all the right places, her body toned like she worked out daily. Not muscular, but firm and trim. Her titties were big round globes with large dark areolas and nipples. DDs was my guess. Her stomach was flat with the outline of a six pack. Her waist was small, hips wide, thighs thick and strong. Her pussy was shaved, the lips nice and plump. After the women checked out each other's bodies, they sat on the couch, kissing and rubbing between one another's thighs.

"Your sexy ass got me so wet," Tracy moaned.

"Let me taste you," Sheila purred, dipping her fingers into Tracy's pussy and tasting the juice. "Mmmm! You taste so sweet!"

My dick was so hard that it felt like it was going to bust! I watched as Tracy stood in front of Sheila, spreading her legs like she was being searched by TSA. Sheila slid to the edge of the couch, parting the fleshy lips of Tracy's pussy and slipping a finger inside.

"Oh shit!" Tracy breathed. "Lick my pussy while you finger me."

Sheila leaned forward and gave Tracy some tongue while jamming two fingers in and out of her hole.

"Oh yes, Sheila! That shit feels so good!" Tracy moaned, tilting her head back and closing her eyes.

Sheila got more into the act, pressing her mouth against Tracy's clit and sucking. In her sexual bliss, Tracy clutched Sheila's head, forcing her mouth harder against her clit. She looked to be nearing her orgasm as she put one foot on the couch, spreading her legs more, allowing Sheila more access to her pussy.

"Yes! Yes!" Tracy cried, clinging to Sheila's head and grinding on her face. "Don't stop! That's perfect! Don't stop!"

Hearing Tracy cum and watching her body shake took me to another level of horniness. I wanted to join them so bad that my dick started to hurt. I unzipped my fly, freeing my shit and began stroking myself while watching the hot lesbian sex scene. Tracy got on her knees, arching her back and poking her big perfect ass in the air as she knelt between Sheila's legs. Her pussy lips poked out the back, slick with the juices from her orgasm. I wanted to go over and slide my dick so far inside of her, but I wasn't a rapist. She said no and I had to respect that.

"Mmm, yeah!" Sheila moaned as Tracy went to work.

She kissed Sheila's pussy crack before running her tongue up and down the slit. Then she parted the lips, exposing Sheila's pink inner folds and clitoris.

"Your pussy is so beautiful and it tastes so good," Tracy said right before sticking two fingers deep into Sheila's guts.

"Oh yeah, Tracy! Eat me while you finger me," Sheila moaned.

Tracy began to kiss and lick Sheila's inner thighs while fingering her.

"C'mon, Tracy. Suck my pussy," Sheila begged.

"No. You have to let the orgasm build."

Sheila reached down and began to rub her own clit but Tracy grabbed her wrist.

"No. You'll cum when I say you can cum."

Sheila's hands fell reluctantly to her side. Tracy continued to finger her, slipping her pinky into Sheila's ass.

"Oh God! Yes, Tracy! Oh yes!" Sheila moaned, grabbing her breasts and pinching her nipples.

"You want me to let you cum now?" Tracy asked.

"Yes! Make me cum!"

"You want me to suck your pussy?"

"Yeah! Just do it. Do it now!" Sheila yelled impatiently.

Tracy lowered her head, sucking Sheila's clit into her mouth while continuing to pump fingers in both holes.

Sheila sucked in a deep breath, her orgasm coming on quickly. "Ohh God! Ohhhhhh!" she screamed as her body shook and pussy gushed.

Watching Sheila cum took me over the edge. "Oh shit!" I grunted as sperm shot out of my dick like a geyser.

"Damn, Carl. I see you enjoyed the show." Tracy smiled, wiping Sheila's cum from her face.

I got up and approached her, nut still dripping from my dick and covering my hand. "I did. Now I'm ready to join the fun."

She grabbed the hand with my seed on it and started licking my fingers. "I told you I don't fuck men on the first date," she said while licking my fingers clean.

I reached out a palmed her big-ass booty. "You really gon' do me like this? You really not gon' let me get in them guts?"

She smiled and winked. "I'll take care of you next time. Your girl has some good pussy. You'll be fine until next time."

Sheila got on her knees in front of me and started sucking my dick while I watched Tracy put on her dress.

"Give me your number so I can call you."

"I can't do that."

"How we gon' keep in touch?"

"I'll keep in touch. Have a good night."

I watched that ass bounce to the door, wishing she would stay. But she didn't.

After the door closed, I focused my attention on Sheila's mouth. I was going to fill her throat with so much nut that she was going to have to get her stomach pumped.

CHAPTER 16

I sat in the passenger seat of the stolen Dish Satellite van, nostalgia gripping me as we drove through Joliet, Illinois. Memories of me and Kianna kidnapping the family almost a decade ago played in my head. I had just got out of prison back then, green to the world and blind to so many truths about people. Back then I was so hungry for a meal that I was satisfied with crumbs. Back then I thought $100,000 was a lot of money. Now that I've given away millions, $100,000 was just a drop in a bucket. I also realized that there were things in this world more important than money. Like power. And tonight I was about to make a major move that would hopefully grant me more power than I ever imagined I could get.

I grabbed the walkie-talkie from my lap and held the button. I needed to give orders to my security.

"T-Bird, can you hear me?"

"Loud and clear, boss," the radio cracked.

"Y'all hang back at the end of the block and look out. Me and Getty got it from here."

"Say less, my nigga," the radio cracked before going silent.

I checked the safety on the Glock before tucking it in my overalls. Then I checked my disguise in the mirror. I wore a fake grey beard and glasses.

"How do I look? " I asked as I slipped on my gloves and Dish Satellite hat.

"You look old." Getty laughed as he parked the van in the driveway of a blue and white house.

"So do you," I shot back. "We gotta get in and out as fast as we can. Don't play no games."

Getty gave me a sideways look. "You know I was clearing houses full of terrorists in Fallujah while you was still eating fruit snacks, right? I got it. Is my beard good?" he asked, checking his disguise.

"We good. Let's go."

After he put on his hat and gloves, I grabbed the toolbox and led the way to the house. When we were on the porch, I rang the doorbell and waited.

"It's cameras all over this muthafucka," Getty mumbled.

I stroked my fake beard. "That's what the disguise is for."

"Who is it?" a woman called from inside.

"Dish Satellite services!" I called.

The door opened and a pretty white female came to the screen door. "What's going on, gentlemen? I didn't call for service."

"We're sorry to just show up like this but we need to check the service of yourself dish. We can be in and out in less than five minutes," Getty explained, wearing a smile.

She hesitated.

"If it's not a good time, we can come back later," I cut in. "It'll only take five minutes, but we don't have to do it today. There's another house at the end of the block that we have to check. "

She took the bait. "I don't want to make you guys come back to do a job that will only take five minutes. Might as well get it done. Come in," she said, opening the door.

I took a quick look around the living room as I stepped in the house, checking for signs of guests. Didn't see anyone. I reached in my overalls and pulled out the gun.

"Oh my God!" she panicked.

"Relax. I'm not here to hurt you," I said, keeping my voice calm. "How many people are in this house?"

"Just me and my kids. Please don't hurt us," she begged, on the verge of tears.

"I told you we won't hurt you. I need you to grab your kids and come with us."

"Why? Who do you want? "

I pointed the gun in her face. "I need you to stop asking questions and do what I say. Let's go get the kids."

She had three kids: an eight-year-old girl, and two boys, ages six and three. I led them from the house and into the back of the van. We drove them to a house on the south side of Chicago where my security would keep an eye on them. While Getty got rid of the van, I grabbed a burner phone and stepped on the porch to make a call.

"Yeah," he answered.

"Damon, what's going on, brotha?"

"Who is this?"

"I'm a friend. Check the security footage at your house and then call me back. And make sure you keep this conversation between me and you."

I hung up before he could say another word. The phone rang a few moments later.

"Damon?"

"What the fuck did you do with my family?" he snapped.

"Your family is safe, and I won't touch them as long as you agree to help me."

"What the fuck do you want?"

"I want to meet face to face. Just you and me. Alone. And then we can talk about what I want."

"You know who I work for, don't you? You're making a big fucking mistake."

"I know exactly who you work for. That's why we're having this conversation. Go to the Walmart in Champagne, Illinois. Don't worry about finding me. I'll find you."

"Wait! How do I know my family is still alive?"

I walked in the house and gave the woman the phone. "It's Damon."

"Damon, what's going on, baby?" she cried.

"I don't know. Are you and the kids okay? Did they hurt you?"

"No. We're fine. What did you do? What do they want?"

I grabbed the phone. "Your family is fine. I told you I just want to talk. Get to the Walmart."

***

Damon showed up at the meet before me, which was fine. I planned it to happen like that. I had a lookout in the lot who called me as soon as Damon's Charger showed up. I had my security pull my Cadillac truck beside the black Charger with tinted windows. I climbed out at the same time as Damon. Betrayal lit his eyes when he recognized me.

"You don't look surprised to see me," I said as I approached him.

"I always knew you was a snake, Carl!" He mugged me.

"That explains why you not surprised. Tell me if this surprises you." I grinned, tapping the Escalade's window.

The door opened and Mikey got out.

Damon's eyed almost popped out of his head. "You the one behind this?" Damon accused, looking like he wanted to fuck Mikey up.

"Your family won't be hurt, Damon. That's my word. I'm sorry for scaring them, but that is the only way I could guarantee your cooperation and help."

Damon shook his head, seething with anger. "I can't believe you did this to my family. You wrong, Mikey."

"I know, brotha. But just hear me out. Denzel doesn't know what he's doing. I'm taking over BBC and I want to keep you on my side. Whatever I have to do to make this up to you, I'll do it. But for now, I need you to tell your people to stand down and let us in the mansion."

"And if I don't?" he asked, mugging me. "You're going to kill my family?"

"Your family won't be hurt, Damon. That's my word," Mikey said, begging for Damon's cooperation.

"If you're not going to hurt them, let them go right now."

It was time for me to step in.

"We don't got time for the back and forth and I'm not as nice as Mikey. If you don't do what we said, you gon' have to bury yo' wife and kids. Now what do you want to do?"

Me and Damon had a stare-off, hatred blazing in his eyes.

"If you hurt my family, I will kill you and everybody that you know."

All I could do was smile.

***

We couldn't make the move on Denzel until Mikey got the call from Damon. The call didn't come until almost one in the morning. I was excited by the thought of the look on Denzel's face when I showed up in his house. He lived in a mega mansion inside a gated community. The nigga had security like he was the president, but I had slipped past all of his defenses.

The Escalade glided to a stop in front of Denzel's mansion followed by two Suburbans filled with my people and a white van that I would use for the second part of my plan. I climbed from the Escalade with Mikey while my team followed. There were 13 of us. We followed Mikey up the staircase. Damon met us at the door.

"He in the master bedroom with Cantrell."

I followed Mikey into one of the most elegant mansions I had ever been in. Marble floors, onyx statues, and expensive art caught my eyes. The nigga even had a waterfall in the great room. I left some of my security downstairs while the rest of us followed Mikey and Damon up a marble staircase. At the top of the stairs, we took a left, walking down a long hall. There was a set of doors at the end of the hallway. Damon put a finger to his lips, signaling for us to be quiet as we approached the doors. Music was playing loudly from the room. Prince's "Purple Rain". We walked through the set of doors and down a short hall that led into the master bedroom.

Denzel and Cantrell were on a big-ass bed, both of them naked. Cantrell lay on her back with her eyes closed, palming the back of Denzel's rapidly moving head as he went down on her. When I realized what was happening, I almost threw up. Denzel wasn't eating Cantrell's pussy, but was sucking Cantrell's dick! His fingers were moving in and out of what I thought was Cantrell's ass, but was actually her pussy. Cantrell had a dick and a pussy! It was a hermaphrodite! Quick visions of flirting with Cantrell played in my head. This was what she meant when she told me she wasn't who I thought she was. I pulled out my phone and began recording the scene. Finally sensing our presence, Cantrell opened her eyes.

"Aahhh!" she screamed, wrapping herself in the sheet.

Denzel looked at his man/girl in confusion before turning to see what she was screaming about. Surprise lit his eyes when he seen me, Mikey, Damon, and some of my security in the room. That surprise quickly turned to anger as he jumped up from the bed and started cursing.

"What the fuck are you muthafuckas doing in my house?"

I pulled my pistol, pointing it to his nuts. "I suggest you stop right there before I castrate yo' ass!"

He continued to approach. "Get the fuck outta here or I'll kill all of you."

I pointed my gun at his feet a fired a warning shot.

Pop!

"Another step, and you dead."

He stopped and began mugging Damon and Mikey. "This how you muthafuckas betray me? You bitch-ass niggas wanna bite the hand that fed y'all?"

Neither man spoke, so I did the talking.

"I always thought you seemed a little feminine, but I never expected to walk in and see you sucking a dick, let alone Cantrell's."

He looked at me like I was a piece of shit. "Do you think I give a fuck about you finding out about my sexual appetite? I own this state and everybody in it. I am the most powerful man in Illinois, you fucking peasant."

I nodded. "How do you think the state will feel once they see your deep throat?" I cracked.

He coughed up a loogie and spat on my chest. "Show the video to the whole world, Carl. I don't give a fuck. Nobody can touch me. I'm Denzel Valentine!"

"I was hoping to avoid exposing your secret. Give me the pistol with my prints on it and I'll walk away."

He laughed. "Oh hell no, Carl. I have that gun in safe keeping for situations like this. Go ahead and kill me. Your life will be taken, too. You killed a police officer. You're looking at life. The Feds might even give you the death penalty."

"I didn't expect this to be easy," I said before nodding to Damon. "Shoot Cantrell."

Fear shone on Denzel's face. "Damon, don't do this!"

Damon shook his head. "Sorry, Denzel."

"Non-lethal," I told him at the last moment.

Pop!

"Ahhhh!" Cantrell screamed, grabbing her leg and trying to stop the bleeding.

"I need that gun, Denzel."

"I'm not giving you the gun, Carl. You might as well kill me right now because I'll never give it to you. We're going down together."

"Again," I told Damon.

He fired again, shooting Cantrell in the arm.

"C'mon, Denzel. Save your girl, or boy, whatever it is."

"Fuck you, Carl." He mugged me.

I expected Denzel not to cooperate. He knew that I would kill him after I got the pistol. He was going to be a hard nut to crack, but I was going to show him that all nuts eventually crack.

"Kill her," I told Damon.

"No, Damon!" Cantrell screamed.

He silenced her with a bullet to the face.

"You're going to die for this," Denzel warned.

"As long as you know that you're going first," I said before shooting him in both of his legs.

"Ahh shit!" he yelled, grabbing his legs as he fell to the ground.

"Hold him down," I told my security.

"Get the fuck off me!" Denzel yelled, trying to fight them off. It was no use. The leg wounds had weakened him.

My men each grabbed a limb and pinned him to the ground. I tucked my pistol, pulled a plastic bag from my pocket, and began suffocating Denzel. His face turned blue and he began foaming at the mouth. Right before he was about to pass out, I removed the bag. Denzel choked and sucked in deep gulps of air.

"Where is the gun?"

"Fuck you, Carl," he managed between breaths.

I out the bag over his head again and choked him until he was about to pass out.

"I need that gun, nigga."

"Suck my dick, nigga," he spat.

I suffocated him again. Right before he passed out, I removed the bag. I kept doing it for an hour. Denzel never cracked.

"I think I know where the gun is," Mikey spoke up.

"Don't fuck with me Mikey!" I warned.

"I'm not. I just remembered the house in Aurora. It's——"

"SHUT THE FUCK UP, YOU FUCKING JUDAS!" Denzel roared.

The BBC boss's reaction told me that Mickey spoke the truth.

"I wish you would've remembered that an hour ago, nigga," I said.

"Mikey, I swear to God, you are going to die for this," Denzel threatened. "You're not going——"

I slipped the bag over his head and choked him until he stopped breathing. When Denzel was finally dead, I breathed a sigh of relief. The power was almost mine.

"Alright, fellas. We're done here. Damon, gather all the security on the grounds into the white van so we can leave."

"What about my family?" he asked.

"You did what we asked you to do. Load the security into the van and I'll take you to them."

When Damon left the room, I turned to my security. "Wire the house and blow it. Leave no evidence."

When everyone was loaded into vehicles, we left the mansion ablaze as we left the gated community and headed for the highway. About thirty minutes into the drive I pulled out a detonator. I checked out the back window to make sure the white van with Damon and his team was still following us. Then I pressed the button.

KABOOM!

The night turned bright as the van was torn in half by the explosion. Then I called Getty and told him to kill Damon's family.

I was about to be the boss of all bosses!

CHAPTER 17

After dispatching Denzel and his security, we headed for the house in Aurora, Illinois. It was located in a good neighborhood where crime wasn't a problem. The house didn't have guards, only a security system that Mickey knew the codes to deactivate. There was no furniture in the house. No traces that anyone had lived here recently. I followed Mikey to a bedroom at the back of the house. Near the closet was a false floor. Mikey lifted a few boards and pulled out a safe. I held my breath in anticipation as he put in the combination, praying the gun was inside because Denzel was dead and there was no other way to get the gun back.

When the safe opened, Mikey smiled.

"Is it in there?" I asked, my heart thudding like it was going to explode.

Mikey reached in and pulled out and Ziploc bag. Inside was the black .9mm Smith & Wesson I used to kill Officer Cooper.

"Give it to me!" I yelled, snatching the bag from his hand. I was finally free! "What else is in there?"

Mikey laughed as he pulled a bunch of manila envelopes from the safe. "Denzel had dirt on a lot of people. Judge O'Flaherty likes to convince people that he's a staunch conservative, but he is secretly apart of the LBGTQ community. D.A. Chisholm likes underage girls. The chief of police——"

I cut him off. "Who else knows about this house and what's in the safe?"

"Nobody. Just me and you."

"Good. We're going to keep this house. Bring those files so I can get familiar with the secrets of our new friends."

When we were back in the truck, I directed my security to the nearest store so I could get some Clorox wipes. During the drive, I went through the folders and learned that Denzel had dirt on lots of high ranking officials in the city. That's how BBC got so powerful and were so protected. And now I held all the power. After getting the Clorox wipes, we went back to the safehouse. While Mikey put the folders back in this floor, I used the wipes to clean my DNA from the gun.

"We really did it, Carl. Denzel is gone. BBC is ours!" Mikey smiled. "You're a genius, man. I owe you my life, brah."

"I told you we could do it." I grinned. "But there is one last thing."

Questions swirled in his eyes. "What else?"

I dropped the bleach cleaned Smith & Wesson on the floor and pulled my own pistol.

"What the fuck you doing, Carl?" Mikey asked, the fear of his worst nightmare coming to life showing in his eyes.

"Pick up the gun and give it to me," I ordered.

He looked confused. "C'mon, Carl. We're in charge. I'm making you my second in command."

I lifted the gun to his face. "I don't want to be second in command. The early bird gets the worm, but the second mouse gets the cheese. Pick up the gun."

He looked like he wanted to cry. "I should've known you didn't do this for me," he lamented, shaking his head. "You don't need my prints on the gun for me to cooperate. You can lead. I won't fight you for it."

"Pick up the gun," I repeated. "You got five seconds."

He looked in my eyes to see how serious I was. "C'mon, Carl. You can have it. I don't want to be in charge."

I began the countdown. "5. 4. 3. 2——"

"Okay!" he yelled, bending down to pick up the gun.

I opened the Ziploc bag for him drop it inside.

"That wasn't personal, Mikey. Just business. I needed an insurance policy."

Betrayal and anger shone in Mikey's eyes. "The second mouse gets the cheese."

"That's right." I nodded. "I'm glad you understand. Call a team meeting so we can explain the transfer of power. Just the soldiers. Leave the big wigs out. I'll talk to them on my own."

***

It took less than forty-eight hours for Mikey to set up a meeting with the BBC soldiers. There were twenty-five of them. We met in an abandoned parking garage, using the cars to form a circle. Everyone leaned against their vehicles, waiting. I watched the soldiers' demeanor and body language. Everyone knew Denzel was dead and had already figured what the meeting was about. And then there was Duke, the alderman's nephew that tried to clip me off downtown. He shot a couple of mean looks my way. I couldn't wait to see the look on his face when he found out I was his boss.

"A'ight, y'all. We ain't gon' make this a long drawn out meeting. I know we all got things to do and I'ma let y'all get back to it," Mikey spoke up. "I know everybody heard about Denzel by now. It's true. Somebody got him. We still looking for who did it and it's a million dollars for anybody that can help us find who killed my nigga."

"How did they get past all the security?" a nigga named Lidel asked.

"We don't know. We think it was an inside job."

"I heard they found all his security blown up on the highway," Amur cut in.

"That's right," Mikey confirmed. "Damon and all them. Like I said, we still tryna put all the pieces together. And we will."

"It seems clear to me," Duke spoke up. "Denzel was the smartest nigga I knew. Only somebody he trusted could get close enough to kill him. He didn't trust none of us. I think the only person he trusted was you."

The accusation hung in the air like a dark raincloud as Duke and Mikey had a stare down.

"What the fuck is you saying, nigga?" Mikey asked, walking upon Duke. "You tryna say I killed my brother, nigga? You accusing me?"

Duke didn't fold under Mikey's display of anger. "I'm just saying what everybody else thinking but won't say."

Mikey mugged Duke before turning to Lucky. "Is that what everybody's thinking? That I killed my brother?"

Lucky turned his head, remaining silent.

Mikey walked up to Amur. "Is that what you think? Huh?"

Amur lowered his head as he spoke. "I didn't say it was you, but I think Duke got a point. Whoever did it was close to him."

Mikey walked in the middle of the room and let his eyes sweep around the soldiers. "Let me tell you niggas something. Denzel was my nigga. We go back over thirty years. Before some of y'all was born. I knew that nigga since we was tikes. We was like brothers. I loved that nigga and I would never betray him. I didn't have no reason. I am BBC. I created this. And him dying didn't change my position. I'm still second in command."

The soldiers looked confused.

"So who the boss now?" Duke asked.

I stepped into the middle of the circle. "I am."

The soldiers started yelling and cursing.

I pulled my pistol and fired a shot in the air.

"Everybody calm down and listen!" I yelled. When they quieted down, I spoke again. "I am the leader of BBC."

"Mikey, what is this about?" Flex asked.

"Denzel was grooming Carl to take his spot if something ever happened to him. Denzel must've seen something in Carl, because he chose him over me. I don't like it, but I'm following orders."

Duke let out a sarcastic laugh. "What, this supposed to be some kind of coincidence? Am I the only one that can see what the fuck happened?"

I lifted my pistol and started shooting Duke until he was on the ground bleeding from several bullet holes. Then I walked over and kneeled next to him, looking him in his eyes. "Insubordination will not be tolerated and is punishable by death!"

He blinked several times, the fear of death showing in the whites of his eyes. Then I lifted the gun to his forehead and took that fear when I pulled the trigger. After taking care of Duke, I stood to face my soldiers.

"I didn't choose this for myself. Denzel did. And I will honor his memory by doing what he asked me to do. I am the leader of the Black Billionaires Cartel. Insubordination is punishable by death."

CHAPTER 18
Six months later

I did it!

I had finally reached my destiny. I, Carlile White, had become the boss of all bosses! I owned one of the biggest cities in America. I was bigger than the mayor of Chicago and the governor of Illinois. I had everyone in my pocket. The district attorney, the police chief, businessmen, federal agents, and judges. I was untouchable. I had left the rank and file of mere human beings and become a god!

"We have power in our words. With our words, we can create and destroy. Our creator gave us this power, but only a few realize this truth and are able to tap into it," I explained to Rachel.

The busty twenty-five-year-old was one of the women hired for entertainment. She had been worshipping me from the moment she stepped foot in my mansion. After several drinks and snorting copious amounts of cocaine up our nostrils, we went to the master bedroom on the second floor and stepped out onto the balcony. There was a full moon high in the sky, illuminating the five wooded acres surrounding my mansion.

"Our creator bestowed upon us the power to be gods, Rachel. We can do miracles but only if you believe. Do you believe, Rachel?"

"I believe, Carl! You are my god and I believe you," she slurred, looking at me like I was the black Messiah.

I leaned close to her ear and whispered, "You can fly, Rachel. You can fly!"

She walked to the edge of the balcony, leaning on the railing and lifting her arms out to her side like an airplane. She wore a white bra, lace panties, and heels. While she was pretending to fly, I walked up behind her, opening my robe and grinding my dick against her ass.

"You can fly, Rachel. Spread your wings and like an eagle and fly. Close your eyes and picture yourself gliding in front of the full moon. Fly higher! Higher! Higher!"

"I'm flying, Carl! I'm flying!" she moaned like she was having an orgasm.

"Fly off the balcony, Rachel! Believe! Fly! Believe!"

And then I gave her a shove.

"Ahhhh!" she screamed.

Instead of going up, she went down, hitting the ground with a sick thud.

"Carl, what the fuck you do?" Sandman asked, running to the edge of the balcony and looking over.

Rachel's body lay twisted on the ground forty feet below.

"Did you see her fly?" I asked, climbing onto the railing.

"She didn't fly, nigga! She dead," he said, pulling out his walkie-talkie. "Getty, check the backyard. A woman fell off the balcony."

"I'm on my way," the radio squawked.

"I seen her fly. Watch me fly," I said, getting ready to jump.

"What the fuck you doing!" Sandman yelled, grabbing my arm and pulling me back to the ground. "You tripping, nigga. You can't fly. Who the fuck you think you is?"

I got in his face, our noses almost touching. "I'm a god, nigga!"

From the balcony, I went through the master bedroom and into the hallway to take the elevator downstairs. Sandman followed, doing his best to protect me from harm. We walked into the great room where a lingerie party was in full swing. I'd invited all of the city's big wigs as well as hired a fleet of escorts to serve me and my colleagues. The women walked around in next to nothing, entertaining the powerful men. I walked into the room with my robe open, dick swinging from side to side. A bad Asian woman sitting on the couch with a federal court judge seen my dick and couldn't take her eyes off of it. That's where I went.

"Good evening, Your Honor," I greeted the judge.

He looked startled to see my robe open. "Hey, Carl. You look like you're having a good time."

"I am." I smiled, winking at this Asian woman. "But what would make me feel even better is her lips wrapped around my dick."

"There are a lot women here, Carl. Jeannie and I are forming a deep connection," the judge said, reaching out and grabbing the woman's hand.

I looked at the judge and laughed. Then I put a hand on top of Jeannie's head and thrust my hips forward, my dick inches from her face. She let go of the judge's hand to grab my dick and put it in her mouth. The judge snarled at me before getting up and walking away. I laughed before closing my eyes and enjoying the blow job.

"Carl?"

I opened my eyes at this sound of Sheila's voice. She walked towards me looking like she just stepped off a Victoria's Secret fashion runway Show. She wore red lingerie, heels, and a pair of angel wings like the women in the fashion show.

"Hey, baby. I don't know her name yet, but she know how to suck dick." I groaned.

Sheila walked over and pulled my dick from my new friend's mouth. "I'm sorry to disturb your blow job, but there is somebody here to see you. And trust me, you really want to see this person."

I tried to read her face. "Who is it?"

A twinkle shone in her eyes and she smiled. "You'll see."

She held onto my dick, leading from the great room and into the foyer. My dick jumped when I seen my fantasy girl standing near the door wearing a white robe.

"It looks like I showed up just in time." Tracy smiled.

"Did I ever tell you that you remind me of Megan Thee Stallion?"
"

"I heard that a time or two. Looking at you, I feel overdressed," she said while taking off the robe. She wore a white bra that had her titties sitting up high, lace panties, and a garter belt with white pantyhose and heels. "How do I look?" she asked, doing a twirl.

I walked up to her, palming those big ass cheeks and sticking my tongue in her mouth. We moved up against the wall. I reached down, opening her legs and pushing her panties aside. I was ready to fuck.

"Wait, Carl." Tracy stopped me, grabbing hold of my dick.

"Wait for what?"

"Let me in this house. This is a party, right? Can I have a drink? Where are the libations? Show me around."

Normally I wouldn't let a female stop me from doing what I wanted to do because no one told gods what to do. But there was something about Tracy that told me she wasn't average. She had an aura similar to Kianna's. A woman that knew her place, worth, power and demanded respect.

"My bad," I apologized, backing away. "You do something to me. Let me show you around and get you a drink."

After getting her a strawberry daiquiri, I took her on a tour of the mansion. We ran into Mikey down in the game room. He was playing pool with a few women. What got my attention was their attire. He only wore boxers, his robe and T-shirt on the floor. One of the women was naked. The other had on one high heel and panties, no bra.

"What's going on, Mikey?"

"Strip pool," he grinned before looking to Tracy. They exchanged a look.

"Now it makes sense." I nodded. "You know her?"

He shook his head. "No, but I would like to."

I pulled Tracy and Sheila close. "These are off limits."

"Cuffing season, huh?"

"Like a grocery bag."

After showing her the movie theatre, I took the women to the master bedroom and out onto the balcony.

"This is nice," Tracy commented, walking to the edge of the balcony and looking out over the moonlit woods.

I stood next to her, glancing down to check for Rachel's body and happy to find her gone. "Where have you been, Tracy? Why didn't you keep in touch?"

She looked at me and smiled. "I told you I would contact you. And I did. That's why I'm here."

"I looked for you but couldn't find you. I hired people. Professionals. They said you don't have a digital fingerprint. Almost like you don't exist."

She smiled again, some kind of dangerous and sexy thing showing in her eyes. Then she closed the distance between us, breasts on my chest, lips close enough to kiss. "You know that I exist. I'm standing right here, ain't I?"

I wanted to stick my tongue in her mouth and start fucking her on the balcony, but first I needed some answers. "How did you find out where I live?"

She looked towards Sheila. "I found her. I had her number all along. I wanted to see you on my terms."

I lifted my hand and grabbed her by the throat. I didn't choke her, but I kept a firm grip. "Why are you being so mysterious?"

She reached inside my robe and grabbed my dick as a sexy and dangerous fire flared behind her brown eyes. "Because you can't have me, Carl. I don't belong to nobody. I want to be in control. Being in control turns me on and gets my pussy wet. And so does choking me. Squeeze harder."

I put pressure on her throat. She responded by squeezing my dick. Shit hurt so I choked her some more, squeezing as hard as I could. She continued squeezing my dick until she started getting weak. She let go of my shit and grabbed my wrist, gasping for air. I was so intoxicated with power and lust that I continued choking her. I literally had her life in my hand and it felt exhilarating.

"Carl, let her go!" Sheila yelled.

The scream brought me back from the dark and murderous place and I let Tracy go. "My bad. Damn."

Tracy leaned against the railing, holding her neck and catching her breath, all the while looking in my eyes.

"What the fuck is wrong with you, Carl?" Sheila snapped at me before checking on Tracy. "Are you okay?"

After a couple of grunts and clearing her throat, Tracy found her voice. "I'm good. That was so close. It's like the closer I get to death, the hornier I get. Feel my pussy. I'm so wet."

Sheila didn't miss a beat. She got on her knees, slid Tracy's panties to the side, and started attacking her pussy. Tracy put a hand on my shoulder and lifted a leg onto the railing to give Sheila better access to her pussy. When I stepped closer, Sheila stopped eating Tracy to give me some head. Then she took turns sucking my dick and eating Tracy's pussy. After a few moments I got tired of the teasing and was ready for action. We went to the room where Sheila lay on her back in bed. Tracy climbed between her legs, on her hands and knees, and starting sucking Sheila's pussy. I climbed behind Tracy and slipped my dick into some of the best pussy I ever felt. I put the pound down, slapping her big ass cheeks while beating the pussy up. When I felt my nut building, I slowed down and we changed positions. Tracy got on top of me and started riding while Sheila sat on my face. When I felt Tracy's hand wrap around my throat, I didn't give it much thought because I was loving the threesome. Until she started squeezing. I tried to pry her hand loose but she used her other hand and wrapped them both around my throat and squeezed harder. I grabbed her wrists, trying to snatch her hands away but Tracy was strong. She rode my dick like a maniac while choking me. It felt like I was about to pass out and my nut was building at the same time.

"Let him go!" Sheila screamed, grabbing Tracy's wrist.

Tracy didn't let go. I could see murder and lust in her eyes as she continued slamming her pussy down on my dick. I was right on the verge of passing out when I busted my nut. The shit felt incredible! I never imagined feeling so good being close to death. My whole body tingled with pleasure.

"Let him go! Sandman, help!" Sheila screamed.

Tracy finally let me go. I coughed, slobbed, and gasped for air as my dick spasmed inside her pussy. Through my painful coughs, Tracy kept riding me, her eyes wide with excitement and lust. She was beyond crazy, and I kind of liked it.

"What's going on?" Sandman yelled, charging into the room.

I lifted a hand, waving him off. "I'm good," I whispered, barely able to talk.

He looked at Sheila's naked body and Tracy still riding me. "Y'all good?"

"We good," I said a little stronger.

"I'm sorry," Sheila apologized, looking embarrassed. "It got a little out of hand."

He looked unsure of what he should do so he shrugged and left the room.

I sat up and wrapped a hand around Tracy's throat. "You ever do that shit again and I'ma kill yo' ass!"

She continued to rock her hips as she rode me, her eyes lowering into angry sexy slits. "I dare you."

***

I woke up the next morning with a sore throat and a hangover. Tracy was gone and Sheila was passed out next to me. The phone ringing was what woke me up. I grabbed it to check the screen. It was Mikey.

"Yeah," I answered, barely able to talk.

"Get up. Feds got the shipment. Shit's crazy at the dock."

My eyes shot open. "What? The Feds? How? Why didn't we know about this?"

"That's what we have to find out. I'm on my way to Chicago right now. Get up."

I jumped out of bed so fast that I got a head rush and almost passed out. After steadying myself and getting my balance, I ran to my closet to get dressed. After waking my security, we hopped in the Cadillac truck and headed downtown. I called Mikey and told him where to meet me. His purple Bentley showed up a few minutes after I got to the spot. I got on him as soon as he got in the truck.

"Tell me what you know."

"Our people were waiting for the freight container. When the crane took it off the boat, we grabbed it. Before they could leave the yard, the Feds got 'em. One of them was able to call my boy, Bam. He called me."

I hung my head and began massaging my temples. A big headache was coming. "2000 pounds of my dope is gone. How come we didn't know about this before it happened? We have people in the federal building. We have police. We have judges and district attorneys. How come we didn't see this coming?" I snapped.

"I'm trying to figure it out. I can't reach Bobby."

"Who the fuck is Bobby?"

"Bobby Ralston is our federal agent with the ATF."

"Call him again. And keep calling him until he answers. Matter of fact, take me to his house. Where does he live?"

Mikey's phone rang, interrupting my rant. He checked this screen and then looked to me. "Speaking of the devil."

I snatched the phone. "Bobby!"

"Hey, Mikey. I just found——"

"This is not Mikey. This is Carl. Where are you?"

"Um... I'm working."

"Where are you? Exact location. We need to talk."

"Now isn't a good time. I had to step away to make this call."

"Tell me where the fuck you are, Bobby! I'm not asking any-more."

"Fuck, Carl," he breathed. "Michigan in twenty minutes."

***

Bobby was tall and stocky with the swagger of a street nigga, but spoke like a white man.

"I'm just as surprised as you are. I was out of the loop on this one. I don't know how I was left out of the bust or why. I was trying to figure that out when you called."

I stared at the Fed with contempt and disgust in my eyes. I wanted to kill him but I still needed him. "I want to know who the agent that was in charge of the raid. Find out where he lives. I want my dope back."

Bobby laughed. "C'mon, Carl. It's a wrap. They're already do-ing the paperwork. You can't get anything back once we get it and start processing it."

I continued my serious stare. "I'm not playing, Bobby. I want to know who the muthafucka is that took my dope."

The smile disappeared from his face. "C'mon, Carl. I can't——"

I pulled my pistol and pointed it in his face. "If you don't get me what I want, your services will no longer be needed."

He nodded. "I'll see what I can do."

"Don't see what you can do. Do it."

"I'll get you the information."

I put my pistol down and nodded towards the door. "Time is of the essence."

"I'll call Mickey as soon as I get the information," he said before climbing from the truck.

"We're not going to be able to get that shipment back. I say we cut our losses before we make it worse," Mikey said.

"And I say differently. Two and a half million dollars' worth of dope is worth every life in the federal building."

J-Blunt

CHAPTER 19

After leaving the meeting with the federal agent, I made the dreadful call to my supplier. Juan Carlos was the leader of the Dominguez cartel in Columbia.

"Carlito! How is my new amigo? Did you get the box?"

"That's why I'm calling. The box didn't make it. Feds."

"Wait, wait, wait, Carlito. You say they got the box?"

"Yeah. It's gone. I need a new one."

"Son of a bitch!" he cursed angrily. "Everything is on hold for now. I will send somebody to speak to you in a couple of days."

Click.

"Wait! Juan Carlos? Juan Carlos?"

"What did he say?" Mikey asked.

I dropped the phone in my lap, struggling to control my anger. "Muthafucka hung up on me. Said he'll send somebody in a couple of days. Who the fuck does he think he is hanging up in my face? I'm not a fucking worker."

"I don't think he meant to disrespect you," Mikey defended. "I know Juan Carlos, and he's not that kind of man. Hearing the Feds got the shipment might've spooked him."

"I don't give a fuck how spooked he is. Hanging up in a man's face is disrespectful. Whoever he sends better have a thousand kilos or I'm flying to Columbia."

***

It took a couple hours for Bobby to find the information on the man in charge of the raid that took my dope. The agent's name was Special Agent Tommy Franklin. He was a forty-four-year-old white man that had been with the ATF for fifteen years. He was well known and respected amongst his colleagues. For him and his family's sake, I hoped that common sense would outweigh his obligation to the federal government, because I would kill everybody standing in the way of getting my dope.

"He's here," my walkie-talkie cracked.

I checked my watch as I looked towards the end of the block. Tommy's blue Ford F-150 entered the cul-de-sac at 10:48 PM. I was sitting in a car near the end of the block. When the truck drove by, I nodded to Getty. "Follow him home."

Getty made the U-turn and headed for the agent's house. By the time we pulled up, Tommy was standing in the middle of the lawn with his hands in the air. There were three green dots on his chest and one on his forehead. My killers were hiding in bushes and on the sides of houses dressed in black and wearing masks.

"Tommy, Tommy, Tommy!" I sang while climbing from the back seat of the Benz wearing a Barack Obama mask.

"Who the fuck are you?" he cursed, anger lighting the middle aged white man's eyes.

I pointed to my Barack Obama mask. "Can't you see I'm the president? We'll talk more inside if you don't mind."

"I'm a federal agent. You're making a huge mistake. Whatever this is, it's not happening."

I got close to him, pointing my pistol into his face while my men frisked him. They took his wallet, keys, phone, and gun. "Oh yes, this is happening. The way I see it, you have two choices. We can go in your house and talk, hopefully coming to an agreement. Or, I can have you killed on your front lawn and then have my men finish your family. Your choice."

We had a brief stare-off. I won.

"Okay. We'll talk. I need my keys."

I nodded to my security. Tommy got the keys and walked upon the porch and began unlocking the door.

"Make sure you reset the alarm," I warned, following him into the house.

He gave a sneer while punching in the code. "What do you want?"

"Your cooperation," I told him before turning to my men. "Find the family."

"Hey! Wait! Leave them alone!" he yelled.

I slapped him in the face with my pistol, knocking him to the floor. "No hero shit, Tommy. I'm here for one reason. I want my damn dope back."

Recognition lit his eyes. "Who are you?"

"I ask the questions, Tommy. How did you find out about the freight container?"

A woman's scream grabbed his attention. "Jenny!" he yelled, attempting to get up from the floor.

I kicked him in the ribs. "Stay there, Tommy. I warned you about the hero shit."

My security dragged a middle-aged black woman and teenage boy into the living room, throwing them on the couch and holding them at gunpoint.

"Tommy, what's going on?" the woman cried.

"Its fine, honey. We'll be okay," Tommy said, trying to comfort his family.

"And you will keep your word to your family, as long as you help me. Tell me how you found out about the freight container."

"It was a tip, man. Somebody called because they seen something that didn't look right."

"You expect me to believe that bullshit?"

"It's the truth, man. I swear to God on my life. We're trying to find out who the shipment belongs to. Your people, the drivers, aren't talking."

I filed what he said in this back of my mind. "I want my dope back. Where is it?"

He let out a sarcastic grunt. "It's in the federal building. It's one of the biggest cocaine busts in Chicago's history. You can't get that back unless the director of the ATF releases it. After he's not going to do that."

"The head of the ATF, huh?" I asked. "So, I guess you're no use to me then."

"Wait! Wait! I can——"

Pop, pop! Two bullets in this forehead silenced this fed.

"Tommy! Nooo!" Jenny screamed.

I nodded to my security. "Finish them."

***

Three days later I was sitting in Irene's along with Mikey having dinner with Senator Aaron Prime. We were discussing the possibility of contributing to his campaign for reelection.

"I want to get to the point, Senator, if you don't mind. I don't have a problem donating to your campaign for reelection. The state of Illinois loves you and I love seeing people that look like me have the power to make important decisions affecting the city of Chicago and state of Illinois," I said. "But I would like to know what you plan on giving me in return."

He smiled like he was expecting the question. "Well, Carl, it depends on the amount of the donation. This agreement is quid pro quo. One hand washes the other. If you help me, I will help you."

It was my turn to smile. "Here is my price, Senator. I will donate five million dollars to your campaign. In return, I need you to set up a meeting with the director of the ATF."

He looked surprised. "Five million dollars just for you to meet with that director of the ATF? What's the catch?"

"Not just to meet with him, but I want you to convince him to join us."

The senator's face went flush, his eyes getting wide as full moons. "Do you realize what you're asking? You want me to convince the head of a federal agency to meet with you to discuss a partnership? I'll have to expose myself. If he doesn't agree, I'll be finished and sitting in a cell."

"Sometimes great progress involves taking calculated risks," I said, checking my phone as it rang. The number was from overseas. "Give me a moment to take this. Hello?"

"Carlito?"

"Yeah. Who is this?"

"Jamie. Juan Carlos sent me to speak with you."

I perked up, suddenly no longer interested in the meeting with the senator. My dope was here. "Okay. Where are you?"

"I'm at O'Hare Airport. I need a ride."

"I'm on the way," I said before ending the call.

"You leaving?" Aaron asked, concern lighting his eyes.

"I have someone waiting for me at the airport," I announced as I stood. "But my offer still stands. Take some time to think about it. I want you to be reelected and I need to meet with the director of the ATF. Set up the meeting. Mikey can stay here and work out the details, but I have to go."

***

I kept my eyes peeled for a brown-skinned man in a salmon colored shirt and white pants as Getty pulled the Cadillac truck to a stop in front of the airport. The bright shirt wasn't hard to find.

"Over there," I pointed, climbing from the truck and waving a hand.

"Carlito!" the Columbian smiled, shaking my hand as he got in the truck.

"Good to meet you, Jamie. How was the flight?"

"Fine. I'm staying at the Hilton. Will you take me there so I can check in?"

"You're staying?" I questioned. "Why? And where is the shipment?"

"I don't have a shipment. I came to talk. Juan Carlos sent me to find out how the Feds captured the shipment. We have done business with Denzel for many years with no interceptions. We have a lot of questions."

I tried to contain my frustration. "The Feds got a tip. That's all I know. Why didn't he send more merch?"

"There is no merch, Carl. Juan Carlos wants me to speak with Mikey. Is he around?"

"Mikey? Why does he want you to talk to Mikey?"

He looked men square in the eyes. "We are familiar with Mikey. We do not know you."

My anger took over. "I am the head of BBC, not Mikey! If Juan Carlos has questions, he can ask me in person. Stop the truck, Getty!"

When the truck stopped, I opened the door, grabbed Jamie, and pushed him out. "Get the fuck out!"

"Hey! C'mon, Carlito! You are making a big mistake."

"I don't make mistakes, I make money," I snapped, closing the door in his face. "Getty, take me to my jet. We're flying to Columbia."

Getty spun in the seat to face me. "Columbia?"

"Yeah. We about to pay Juan Carlos a visit."

"We probably need Jamie for this one. The cartels control Columbia. If we don't have someone that knows their way around, we might get in trouble."

I let out a hot breath. He was right. When I opened the door, Jamie was still standing there. "Get in the truck. We're going to pay your boss a visit."

Before going to the airstrip where my G6 was parked in a hanger, I went to get extra ammunition. I had a feeling I would need it.

CHAPTER 20

If I would've flown to Columbia without Jamie, me and my team would've gotten lost, ended up in jail, or killed. I didn't know a damn thing about the country or speak Spanish. But because I flew in with the kingpin's errand boy, I was allowed into the country and treated like a foreign diplomat.

Medellin, Columbia was in the northern part of South America. During the fly-over I got a glimpse of the Amazon rainforest. Medellin was a big city with skyscrapers and nice houses. The outskirts of the city was where they housed the poor in fucked up shanty houses.

After landing at a small private airport, I waited in the hanger while Jamie went with some of my security to rent SUVs. Jamie wanted to call Juan Carlos to let him know we were coming, but I denied the request. I wanted my visit to be a surprise. When three SUVs with tinted windows pulled into the hanger, I got off the private jet with eight heavily-armed members of my security. I heard stories of massacres in Medellin. Drug cartels could turn any area of the city into a war zone at any moment, so I came ready. As we were leaving the small airport, we drove by a convoy of SUVs parked near the front of the car rental agency. Several Columbians stood outside the vehicles holding choppers, watching our SUVs with great interest.

"Who are they?" I asked Jamie.

"They are The Imperials, a rival cartel."

"They acted like they wanted to make a move on us when we was renting the trucks," Getty said.

"Should we be concerned?" I asked Jamie.

"If you were alone, yes. But they won't touch you while you're with me. Juan Carlos would wipe them off the face of the earth."

Hearing how powerful my connect was allowed me to relax. A little.

We drove highways of Medellin for a while before turning off onto a two lane country road. The ride through the countryside lasted about an hour before we arrived at Juan Carlos's compound.

The estate was on five acres of land surrounded by a big ass twenty foot brick wall. Armed security surrounded the estate and there were several towers with armed men inside. When we pulled up, the security surrounded the vehicles, machine guns ready.

"I need to get out," Jamie said.

I nodded.

He climbed out and began speaking with the security. I didn't know what they were saying, but I noticed one of the men begin speaking into a walkie-talkie. The front gate of the compound opened and more armed men rushed out.

"Shit! Get ready, y'all!" I panicked, pointing my assault rifle at the tinted window. If I went out, I was taking some of them with me.

Getty and the rest of my niggas in the truck got on point. That's when Juan Carlos appeared. He was a short brown-skinned Columbian with a low haircut and clean shaved. He wore a white polo shirt, khaki shorts, and sandals. He said a few words to Jamie before walking to my truck.

"Carlito? Carlito, get out. Where are you?"

I opened the door slowly, holding onto my chopper as I stepped out of the truck.

"Carlito!" Juan Carlos sang, opening his arms and wrapping me in a hug. "How are you, brother?" he asked, patting my back a couple of times, feeling my vest.

"I'm good, Juan Carlos. I'm good."

"I see you've come prepared." He smiled knowingly, patting my vest and eyeing my gun.

"I've heard stories about Columbia."

"Yes. And those stories are probably true." He nodded. Then his face turned serious. "What are you doing here?"

"I want to talk."

He waved at Jamie. "That is why I sent Jamie. I wanted him to speak with Mikey. I've done business with him from many years and I trust him. You, not so much."

"And that's what I wanted to talk to you about. I am the leader of BBC, not Mikey. If you have any questions, I can answer them."

He stared at me for a moment, judging my character and heart. "Okay, Carlito. Come. Bring your men. We can talk inside."

Inside the walls of the compound were more armed men with enough firepower to fight a war. I seen a couple .50 caliber machine guns mounted on top of Humvees, rocket launchers, and two tanks. Now I understood why the Imperials didn't bother us at the car rental agency. I followed Juan Carlos through the compound where he led us to a big ass patio. There were about ten women in bikinis lounging around the furniture. There was also a man present. He stood as we approached.

"Carl, this is my baby brother, Roberto," Juan Carlos introduced. "Ladies, get out of here so I can talk to my friend. Ximena, bring us some bottles of tequila. Carl, have a seat."

After we were seated and the drinks were poured, Juan Carlos began with the questions.

"What happened to the shipment? How did the Feds find it?"

"It was some kind of anonymous tip. The Feds don't know who it belongs to. They have the truck drivers in custody, but they won't talk."

"Are you sure?"

"Yes."

"Why?"

"Because I will kill their whole family. And they know the consequences of insubordination."

"Let's hope so." He nodded. "How did you find out the Feds got a tip?"

"Because I killed the agent that was in charge of the interception. He told me what he knew before he died."

Juan Carlos looked surprised. "You killed a Fed?"

"I tried to get him to work for me, but he wouldn't. He left me no choice."

Juan Carlos and his brother began speaking in Spanish. I watched, wishing like hell I knew what they were talking about. When the conversation carried on longer than I thought it should, I cleared my throat.

Juan Carlos smiled. "Apologies for that, but we are concerned that your business with the Feds could be far reaching. I think we should suspend operations until we are comfortable doing business again."

His words felt like a punch to the gut. "What? I didn't fly halfway across the world to be told that I'm going to have to put my business on hold. You let me worry about the Feds. I can handle it."

He laughed. "I don't think you understand how this works, Carlito. I don't work for you. You work for me. We are not equals. I make the decisions and I say we are putting our business on hold until your situation with this Feds goes away. Okay?"

Me and the kingpin had a stare-off. This muthafucka was actually trying to boss up on me and I wasn't having it. I was my own boss. My own man.

"I said, okay?" Juan Carlos repeated, his brow wrinkling, face scrunching.

I busted out laughing.

"Something funny, Carlito?" Juan Carlos mugged me.

"Let me tell you something, Juan Carlos, so that we are clear. You are not my boss. I don't know what arrangement you had with Denzel, but we don't have that same arrangement. I've killed too many muthafuckas to get here and become my own boss, and I'll be dammed if you are going to talk to me like I'm a worker. You got me fucked up. You are my supplier. That's it. If you have any other impression about this relationship, get that shit out of your head."

Juan Carlos looked at me like I had slapped him. His face turned red and it looked like smoke was coming out of his ears.

"You are in my country! In my house! And you want to talk to me like this? I can kill all of you right now and have your bodies shipped back to America in pieces!"

I laughed again, pulling a detonator from my pocket while he was speaking. Then I began unbuttoning my shirt.

"Oh, you think I am joking!?" Juan Carlos yelled, pulling a pistol from his waist as he stood.

After revealing my explosive vest, I waved the detonator. Realization flashed in Juan Carlos's eyes.

"Yeah, muthafucka!" I grinned, standing with my finger on the trigger. "If I go out, I'm taking half of your compound with me."

Juan Carlos held his hands up. "Okay, papi. You got it. You got it. Take it easy."

I walked towards him and his brother. "I came here to do business and this how you do me? Treat me like a worker and threaten to kill me?"

"Everybody has a place, Carlito. What you are doing is very disrespectful. How you think you gonna make it out of Columbia, huh? This is my country. Medellin is my city. You might as well kill yourself now, because you'll never make it back to America. "

"Wanna bet?" I challenged, grabbing his brother by the arm. "This is my insurance policy. He's coming with me."

Roberto tried to put up a fight. I lifted the detonator. "You ready to die?"

"It's okay, Roberto. Go with him," Juan Carlos said. "This means war, Carlito. And my reach is global."

I grabbed Roberto by the arm and began walking towards the front of the compound. My security surrounded us, leading the way. Juan Carlos walked with us, his small army surrounding my security. The situation was tense, but I knew no one would fire a shot and risk killing the boss or his brother. When we got to the truck, I made sure to sit next to Roberto.

"How we playing this, Carl?" Getty asked as he climbed in the driver's seat.

"To the airport. We gotta get the fuck outta Columbia."

"It doesn't matter where you go. We will find you." Roberto sneered.

I reached my arm back as slapped the shit out of Roberto. "Shut the fuck up!"

When we pulled away from the compound, Juan Carlos followed with five truckloads of men. They followed us all the way to the airport. When I seen The Imperials still parked outside of the car rental agency, I got an idea.

"Getty, pull up on those trucks."

"What are you doing? " Roberto asked nervously.

I ignored him and rolled down the window. "Does anyone speak English?" I asked The Imperials.

A tall brown-skinned man with a curly afro spoke up. "I do. Who are you?"

As he was asking the question, Juan Carlos's convoy pulled up and his men started getting out with weapons. The Imperials got on point and took defensive positions behind their vehicles.

"I'm Carl. I'm from America. Do you know who this is?"

He peered into the truck while keeping an eye on Juan Carlos's men. "Yeah. What do you want?"

"If you help me get out of Columbia, I will give him to you."

He looked confused. "What the fuck are you talking about?"

It was obvious he wasn't in charge of shit. "Juan Carlos is trying to kill me. The only reason he hasn't is because I took his brother hostage. I am a kingpin from America. I want to do business with your boss and I will give him Roberto."

The man looked unsure of what he should do. Another Imperial called out to him and they began speaking in Spanish. Juan Carlos got out of his truck and started yelling at The Imperials. The only thing I understood was the word bomb. Then the Imperial I had been talking to looked at me and smiled.

"Follow us."

All of The Imperials jumped in trucks and pulled away. We followed. Juan Carlos's caravan followed us for about thirty minutes. When we entered a forest, Juan Carlos stopped following. Amongst the trees, I could see armed figures. A quarter mile down the road was a compound. Armed men guarded this front. When the gate opened, we followed The Imperial trucks inside. About twenty armed men stood around the gravel filled parking lot. The Imperials piled from their trucks and the one who spoke English walked up to a tall light skinned Columbian that wore a long ponytail. After the exchange, they walked to my SUV.

"Get out, Carl!" the man with the ponytail called.

I kept the detonator in my hand as I climbed from the truck. My men followed, leaving Roberto inside.

The man with the ponytail looked me over and smiled. "You really have Roberto Dominguez in the truck?"

I nodded. "I do."

He looked at the detonator in my hand. "Where is the bomb?"

I tapped my chest.

Excitement flashed in his eyes. "You have heart. Why did you come to Columbia?"

"I came here to do business with Juan Carlos, but..." I shrugged my shoulders. "Shit didn't work out. Who are you?"

"I am Miguel. Eddie tells me you are a kingpin in America, yes?"

"Yes," I nodded. "I need a new connect. Millions of dollars a month."

Miguel smiled. "Come into my castle and let me officially welcome you to Columbia. Give me Roberto, and I will get you out of Columbia and become your new supplier."

J-Blunt

CHAPTER 21

Hooking up with Miguel made the trip to Columbia worth it. During our meeting, I found out The Imperials were more powerful than Jamie said. They had the manpower, artillery, and money to bring pain to Juan Carlos. Neither of them wanted a war because it would interfere with their money and bring in the Columbian army. So they struck a deal. Miguel got me out of the country safely in return for Roberto to go safely back to his brother. A week later, I got my first shipment from The Imperials. Miguel supplied me with all the dope I needed at the same price Juan Carlos gave it to me. BBC was back like we never left!

"I have a surprise for you," Tracy whispered in my ear.

She was sitting on my lap, looking good enough to eat. Sheila sat next to us, also looking like a snack. We were chilling in the VIP at Litty, a new club in Chicago that everyone was talking about. I was about to talk shit when someone in the crowd caught my eye. Before I could make sure it was her, she vanished. I had to be tripping. No way was she here.

"Get up," I told Tracy, almost shoving her off my lap.

"What happened?"

"I think I just seen somebody," I mumbled, standing to look around.

"Who is it?" Sheila asked.

I ignored my ladies and walked to the VIP ropes to look out over the club. That's when I spotted her again. She stood in the middle of them crowd watching me.

"Kianna," I whispered.

Seeing her made my heart jump. I couldn't believe she was actually here. Feelings of anger, love, and betrayal flooded my body making it hard for me to think. I left the VIP section with my security close behind. Kianna waited for me. When I reached her, we had a face-off, nobody saying a word. But she didn't need to speak for me to understand her. I could read the truth in her hazel brown eyes. Drayez was dead and now she realized her mistake. She was sorry. She loved me. She wanted to come back home. I grabbed her by the arm and led her to the back of the club. My security cleared the way to the back door. When we were outside, I threw her against the building and let my anger take over.

"What the fuck you doing here, Kianna?"

"I didn't have nowhere else to go. Everything that I had is gone. I don't have nothing or no one."

Seeing Kianna so humbled surprised me. She was a proud woman with a high self-worth and self-image. And now she was at my feet begging for a spot in my world.

"Do you expect me to feel sorry for you? You betrayed me. I gave you a chance to make it right but you betrayed me a second time. You let Drayez live. Do you know how much I suffered because of your betrayal? I almost lost everything. And now you expect me to forgive you? Are you crazy?"

"I'm sorry, Carl. My feelings got in the way. I tried to kill him, but I couldn't."

I pulled my pistol.

"Not here, Carl!" Getty yelled, grabbing my arm and pointing to the camera mounted above this club's back door.

"Get the limo."

While Getty went to get the vehicle, the back door opened. Mikey, Sheila, and Tracy walked outside.

"What's going on?" Mikey asked, looking from me to Kianna.

"I'm leaving. I have some business to take care of."

"Who is she?" Sheila asked.

I shook my head while staring in Kianna's eyes. "Somebody that I used to know."

"Are you going to kill me, Carl?" Kianna asked, searching my eyes.

"You deserve to die. You deserve to be buried next to both of your boyfriends, Drayez and Trav."

Mentioning her boyfriends caused her eyes to glow.

"Touched a nerve, huh?" I chuckled.

She shook her head. "Drayez isn't dead."

It felt like I got punched in the chest. "What?"

"Shit!" Tracy cursed, dropping her purse.

I kept my eyes on Kianna as the Hummer limo pulled up. "What did you say? Drayez isn't dead? Where is he?"

"I don't know. But he's not dead."

I was so stunned that I couldn't talk or move. I watched the house explode.

"Carl?" my security called, holding the door open for me to get in the truck.

"Get in," I ordered the women.

When we were in the limousine, I sat across from Kianna, staring in her eyes. She had to be lying. I watched Drayez go in the house. How could he have survived?

"How do you know Drayez is still alive? I watched the house blow up."

"Yes, the house blew up, but he survived. I don't know how, but he did."

"How do you know? Where is he?"

"I know because I talked to him."

"When?"

"She's lying," Tracy cut in.

I mugged her. "Why the fuck are you in my business?"

Tracy looked at Kianna with disgust. "Because she's lying. She knows you are going to kill her and she's buying time. Don't believe her."

"Shut up, Tracy. If I want your opinion, I would ask. Matter of fact, Getty, stop the truck!"

When the Hummer pulled over, I turned to Sheila and Tracy. "Get out. Call Mikey and have him pick y'all up."

Sheila tried to speak. "Wait, Carl, we can——"

"GET THE FUCK OUT RIGHT NOW!" I snapped, pointing my gun at them.

The women opened the door and got out quickly.

"When did you talk to him?" I asked, turning back to Kianna.

"He called about five or six months ago. I haven't heard from him since."

I ran a hand across my face in frustration. I believed Kianna. She had no reason to lie. Drayez was still alive. Fuck!

"Where is he?"

"I don't know. He wouldn't tell me. "

I pointed my gun on her face. "Where the fuck is Drayez, bitch?"

"I don't know. On everything I love, I don't know. If I did, I would tell you."

I searched her eyes for a moment. I wasn't sure if she was telling this truth. She loved Drayez and had already betrayed me to protect him.

"Get on your knees," I ordered.

She maintained eye contact with me as she knelt.

"Open your mouth. "

When her lips parted, I pushed the gun in her mouth.

"Suck it."

Kianna stared in my eyes while her lips moved up and down the barrel of the gun. And then I squeezed the trigger.

Pop!

Kianna's body flew against the seat as the bullet opened the back of her skull, spraying blood on the window. Her eyes remained open, staring at me as she died. I regretted killing her as soon as the life drained from her eyes. She was the only woman I had ever loved. My heart was heavy with grief.

"Take me home, Getty."

I stared into Kianna's lifeless eyes all the way to my mansion. When Getty parked in the driveway, I climbed out.

"Get rid of the body. Make sure it's never found."

"I got you, boss."

I walked in the house and gave orders to my security that I didn't want to be disturbed. Then I went to the master bedroom, closed the door behind me, and fell onto the bed. I had killed a lot of people but I had never felt bad about it until now. I regretted killing Kianna. I loved her. I would always love her. She was the only best friend I ever had. I lay wallowing in grief and memories of Kianna.

Twenty minutes later, there was a knock on the door.

"Carl?" Tracy called.

"I don't want to be bothered. Leave."

"Okay. I'll leave. I just wanted to make sure you were okay and bring you a drink."

I snatched the glass from her hand and downed the drink, hoping the brown liquor would remove the guilt that was building in my chest.

"Do you want me to get you another drink?" she asked.

I shook my head.

"Where is Kianna?"

I couldn't say the words so I shook my head.

"She betrayed you. You did what you had to do."

I let out a long breath. "She was the only woman that I ever loved," I admitted.

Tracy sat next to me and grabbed my hand. "She didn't deserve your love, Carl. Loyalty is love."

"I agree."

We sat in silence for a few moments. Then I started to feel funny. My vision got blurry and I was disoriented. I tried to stand but fell back to the bed.

"What the fuck you do to me?" I mumbled, trying to stand up again.

"You need to calm down, Carl," Tracy said.

I finally got to my feet and stumbled towards the door. I was almost there when gravity escaped me and I fell to the floor. Tracy grabbed me, helping me to my feet.

"Come to bed, Carl. You need to sleep."

"What the fuck you give me, bitch?" I slurred, unable to fight or scream.

"I gave you something to help you relax. Get in bed. Let me help you out of these clothes."

I couldn't do anything but watch as Tracy lay me in bed and began to undress me.

"I'm going to tell you something that is probably going to fuck up your head, Carl. Kianna was right. Drayez is still alive. You wanna know how I know?" she asked, pulling out a knife. "Because Drayez is my little brother. Marie was my mom. You killed her. And now I'm going to kill you."

"No!" I tried to scream but my voice came out as a whisper. "Wait, Tracy. I have to tell you something."

She spread my legs apart. "What do you have to say, Carl?"

"Drayez is my son."

She laughed. "That's funny you should say that, because I already knew. Marie told me. But that ain't going to help you. Nobody's going to help you, Carl. Mikey is downstairs with Sheila and your security. He is the one that helped set this up. You took BBC from him, and he wants it back."

I felt Mikey's betrayal deep in my gut, but it was quickly replaced by the worst pain I ever felt in my life. Tracy pushed the knife between my legs, up into my prostate. I tried to scream, but my voice was gone. All I could do was watch in pain as she pulled the knife from my prostate and begin sawing my dick off. My body exploded with pain as the blood gushed from my loins. Tracy's eyes reflected the joy she got from my torture. When my dick was fully detached, she stuck it in my mouth. Then she brought the knife to my neck. I could feel the blade cut into my throat as she cut from ear to ear. Warm blood poured from the wound and I could taste the blood in my mouth. Then all of a sudden I felt tired. I knew that meant I was dying.

My life began flashing before my eyes. My mom stabbing the whole family before killing herself. The first time I killed somebody on my nineteenth birthday. My brother Chris's face. My niggas Crash's and Rideout's faces as they died. Jewels shooting me after the robbery and the look on his face when I killed him. The day I was released from prison. Meeting Drayez. The look in Kianna's eyes right before she died. And finally my Nana. She wore all white and had the glow of an angel. She was smiling, looking more beautiful than I had ever seen her.

The pain suddenly vanished from my body as I was wrapped up by an indescribably peaceful feeling. Then everything went black.

The End

Submission Guideline

Submit the first three chapters of your completed manuscript to ldpsubmissions@gmail.com, subject line: Your book's title. The manuscript must be in a .doc file and sent as an attachment. Document should be in Times New Roman, double spaced and in size 12 font. Also, provide your synopsis and full contact information. If sending multiple submissions, they must each be in a separate email.

Have a story but no way to send it electronically? You can still submit to LDP/Ca$h Presents. Send in the first three chapters, written or typed, of your completed manuscript to:

LDP: Submissions Dept
Po Box 944
Stockbridge, Ga 30281

DO NOT send original manuscript. Must be a duplicate.

Provide your synopsis and a cover letter containing your full contact information.

Thanks for considering LDP and Ca$h Presents.

Coming Soon from Lock Down Publications/Ca$h Presents

BOW DOWN TO MY GANGSTA

By **Ca$h**

TORN BETWEEN TWO

By **Coffee**

BLOOD OF A BOSS **VI**

SHADOWS OF THE GAME II

TRAP BASTARD II

By **Askari**

LOYAL TO THE GAME **IV**

By **T.J. & Jelissa**

IF LOVING YOU IS WRONG... **III**

By **Jelissa**

TRUE SAVAGE **VIII**

MIDNIGHT CARTEL IV

DOPE BOY MAGIC IV

CITY OF KINGZ III

By **Chris Green**

BLAST FOR ME **III**

A SAVAGE DOPEBOY III

CUTTHROAT MAFIA III

DUFFLE BAG CARTEL VI

HEARTLESS GOON VI

By **Ghost**

A HUSTLER'S DECEIT III

KILL ZONE **II**

BAE BELONGS TO ME III

A DOPE BOY'S QUEEN III

By **Aryanna**

COKE KINGS V

KING OF THE TRAP III

By **T.J. Edwards**

GORILLAZ IN THE BAY V

3X KRAZY III

De'Kari

THE STREETS ARE CALLING II

Duquie Wilson

KINGPIN KILLAZ IV

STREET KINGS III

PAID IN BLOOD III

CARTEL KILLAZ IV

DOPE GODS III

Hood Rich

SINS OF A HUSTLA II

ASAD

KINGZ OF THE GAME VI

Playa Ray

SLAUGHTER GANG IV

RUTHLESS HEART IV

By Willie Slaughter

FUK SHYT II

By Blakk Diamond

TRAP QUEEN

RICH $AVAGE II

By Troublesome

YAYO V

GHOST MOB II

Stilloan Robinson

CREAM III

By Yolanda Moore

SON OF A DOPE FIEND III

HEAVEN GOT A GHETTO II

By Renta

FOREVER GANGSTA II

GLOCKS ON SATIN SHEETS III

By Adrian Dulan

LOYALTY AIN'T PROMISED III

By Keith Williams

THE PRICE YOU PAY FOR LOVE III

By Destiny Skai

I'M NOTHING WITHOUT HIS LOVE II

SINS OF A THUG II

TO THE THUG I LOVED BEFORE II

By Monet Dragun

LIFE OF A SAVAGE IV

MURDA SEASON IV

GANGLAND CARTEL IV

CHI'RAQ GANGSTAS IV

KILLERS ON ELM STREET IV

JACK BOYZ N DA BRONX III

A DOPEBOY'S DREAM II

By **Romell Tukes**

QUIET MONEY IV

EXTENDED CLIP III

THUG LIFE IV

By **Trai'Quan**

THE STREETS MADE ME III

By **Larry D. Wright**

Blood on the Money 3

IF YOU CROSS ME ONCE II

ANGEL III

By **Anthony Fields**

FRIEND OR FOE III

By **Mimi**

SAVAGE STORMS III

By **Meesha**

THE STREETS WILL NEVER CLOSE II

By **K'ajji**

NIGHTMARES OF A HUSTLA III

By King Dream

IN THE ARM OF HIS BOSS

By Jamila

HARD AND RUTHLESS III

MOB TOWN 251 II

By Von Diesel

LEVELS TO THIS SHYT II

By Ah'Million

MOB TIES III

By SayNoMore

THE LAST OF THE OGS III

Tranay Adams

FOR THE LOVE OF A BOSS II

By C. D. Blue

MOBBED UP II

By King Rio

BRED IN THE GAME II

By S. Allen

Available Now

RESTRAINING ORDER **I & II**
By **CA$H & Coffee**
LOVE KNOWS NO BOUNDARIES **I II & III**
By **Coffee**
RAISED AS A GOON I, II, III & IV
BRED BY THE SLUMS I, II, III
BLAST FOR ME I & II
ROTTEN TO THE CORE I II III
A BRONX TALE I, II, III
DUFFLE BAG CARTEL I II III IV V
HEARTLESS GOON I II III IV V
A SAVAGE DOPEBOY I II
DRUG LORDS I II III
CUTTHROAT MAFIA I II
By **Ghost**
LAY IT DOWN **I & II**
LAST OF A DYING BREED I II
BLOOD STAINS OF A SHOTTA I & II III
By **Jamaica**
LOYAL TO THE GAME I II III
LIFE OF SIN I, II III
By **TJ & Jelissa**
BLOODY COMMAS I & II
SKI MASK CARTEL I II & III
KING OF NEW YORK I II,III IV V
RISE TO POWER I II III

COKE KINGS I II III IV
BORN HEARTLESS I II III IV
KING OF THE TRAP I II
By **T.J. Edwards**
IF LOVING HIM IS WRONG…I & II
LOVE ME EVEN WHEN IT HURTS I II III
By **Jelissa**
WHEN THE STREETS CLAP BACK I & II III
THE HEART OF A SAVAGE I II III
By **Jibril Williams**
A DISTINGUISHED THUG STOLE MY HEART I II & III
LOVE SHOULDN'T HURT I II III IV
RENEGADE BOYS I II III IV
PAID IN KARMA I II III
SAVAGE STORMS I II
By **Meesha**
A GANGSTER'S CODE I &, II III
A GANGSTER'S SYN I II III
THE SAVAGE LIFE I II III
CHAINED TO THE STREETS I II III
BLOOD ON THE MONEY I II III
By **J-Blunt**
PUSH IT TO THE LIMIT
By **Bre' Hayes**
BLOOD OF A BOSS **I, II, III, IV, V**
SHADOWS OF THE GAME
TRAP BASTARD
By **Askari**
THE STREETS BLEED MURDER **I, II & III**
THE HEART OF A GANGSTA I II& III

J-Blunt

By **Jerry Jackson**
CUM FOR ME I II III IV V VI VII
An **LDP Erotica Collaboration**
BRIDE OF A HUSTLA **I II & II**
THE FETTI GIRLS **I, II& III**
CORRUPTED BY A GANGSTA I, II III, IV
BLINDED BY HIS LOVE
THE PRICE YOU PAY FOR LOVE I II
DOPE GIRL MAGIC I II III
By **Destiny Skai**
WHEN A GOOD GIRL GOES BAD
By **Adrienne**
THE COST OF LOYALTY I II III
By Kweli
A GANGSTER'S REVENGE **I II III & IV**
THE BOSS MAN'S DAUGHTERS I II III IV V
A SAVAGE LOVE **I & II**
BAE BELONGS TO ME I II
A HUSTLER'S DECEIT I, II, III
WHAT BAD BITCHES DO I, II, III
SOUL OF A MONSTER I II III
KILL ZONE
A DOPE BOY'S QUEEN I II
By **Aryanna**
A KINGPIN'S AMBITON
A KINGPIN'S AMBITION **II**
I MURDER FOR THE DOUGH
By **Ambitious**
TRUE SAVAGE I II III IV V VI VII
DOPE BOY MAGIC I, II, III

174

MIDNIGHT CARTEL I II III
CITY OF KINGZ I II
By **Chris Green**
A DOPEBOY'S PRAYER
By **Eddie "Wolf" Lee**
THE KING CARTEL **I, II & III**
By **Frank Gresham**
THESE NIGGAS AIN'T LOYAL **I, II & III**
By **Nikki Tee**
GANGSTA SHYT **I II &III**
By **CATO**
THE ULTIMATE BETRAYAL
By **Phoenix**
BOSS'N UP **I , II & III**
By **Royal Nicole**
I LOVE YOU TO DEATH
By Destiny J
I RIDE FOR MY HITTA
I STILL RIDE FOR MY HITTA
By **Misty Holt**
LOVE & CHASIN' PAPER
By **Qay Crockett**
TO DIE IN VAIN
SINS OF A HUSTLA
By **ASAD**
BROOKLYN HUSTLAZ
By **Boogsy Morina**
BROOKLYN ON LOCK I & II
By **Sonovia**
GANGSTA CITY

J-Blunt

By **Teddy Duke**

A DRUG KING AND HIS DIAMOND I & II III

A DOPEMAN'S RICHES

HER MAN, MINE'S TOO I, II

CASH MONEY HO'S

THE WIFEY I USED TO BE I II

By Nicole Goosby

TRAPHOUSE KING **I II & III**

KINGPIN KILLAZ I II III

STREET KINGS I II

PAID IN BLOOD **I II**

CARTEL KILLAZ I II III

DOPE GODS I II

By **Hood Rich**

LIPSTICK KILLAH **I, II, III**

CRIME OF PASSION I II & III

FRIEND OR FOE I II

By **Mimi**

STEADY MOBBN' **I, II, III**

THE STREETS STAINED MY SOUL I II

By **Marcellus Allen**

WHO SHOT YA **I, II, III**

SON OF A DOPE FIEND I II

HEAVEN GOT A GHETTO

Renta

GORILLAZ IN THE BAY **I II III IV**

TEARS OF A GANGSTA I II

3X KRAZY I II

DE'KARI

TRIGGADALE I II III

Elijah R. Freeman
GOD BLESS THE TRAPPERS I, II, III
THESE SCANDALOUS STREETS I, II, III
FEAR MY GANGSTA I, II, III IV, V
THESE STREETS DON'T LOVE NOBODY I, II
BURY ME A G I, II, III, IV, V
A GANGSTA'S EMPIRE I, II, III, IV
THE DOPEMAN'S BODYGAURD I II
THE REALEST KILLAZ I II III
THE LAST OF THE OGS I II
Tranay Adams
THE STREETS ARE CALLING
Duquie Wilson
MARRIED TO A BOSS… I II III
By Destiny Skai & Chris Green
KINGZ OF THE GAME I II III IV V
Playa Ray
SLAUGHTER GANG I II III
RUTHLESS HEART I II III
By Willie Slaughter
FUK SHYT
By Blakk Diamond
DON'T F#CK WITH MY HEART I II
By Linnea
ADDICTED TO THE DRAMA I II III
IN THE ARM OF HIS BOSS II
By Jamila
YAYO I II III IV
A SHOOTER'S AMBITION I II
BRED IN THE GAME

J-Blunt

By S. Allen
TRAP GOD I II III
RICH $AVAGE
By Troublesome
FOREVER GANGSTA
GLOCKS ON SATIN SHEETS I II
By Adrian Dulan
TOE TAGZ I II III
LEVELS TO THIS SHYT
By Ah'Million
KINGPIN DREAMS I II III
By Paper Boi Rari
CONFESSIONS OF A GANGSTA I II III
By Nicholas Lock
I'M NOTHING WITHOUT HIS LOVE
SINS OF A THUG
TO THE THUG I LOVED BEFORE
By Monet Dragun
CAUGHT UP IN THE LIFE I II III
By Robert Baptiste
NEW TO THE GAME I II III
MONEY, MURDER & MEMORIES I II III
By Malik D. Rice
LIFE OF A SAVAGE I II III
A GANGSTA'S QUR'AN I II III
MURDA SEASON I II III
GANGLAND CARTEL I II III
CHI'RAQ GANGSTAS I II III
KILLERS ON ELM STREET I II III

Blood on the Money 3

JACK BOYZ N DA BRONX I II
A DOPEBOY'S DREAM
By **Romell Tukes**
LOYALTY AIN'T PROMISED I II
By Keith Williams
QUIET MONEY I II III
THUG LIFE I II III
EXTENDED CLIP I II
By **Trai'Quan**
THE STREETS MADE ME I II
By **Larry D. Wright**
THE ULTIMATE SACRIFICE I, II, III, IV, V, VI
KHADIFI
IF YOU CROSS ME ONCE
ANGEL I II
IN THE BLINK OF AN EYE
By **Anthony Fields**
THE LIFE OF A HOOD STAR
By Ca$h & Rashia Wilson
THE STREETS WILL NEVER CLOSE
By K'ajji
CREAM I II
By Yolanda Moore
NIGHTMARES OF A HUSTLA I II
By King Dream
CONCRETE KILLA I II
By Kingpen
HARD AND RUTHLESS I II
MOB TOWN 251
By Von Diesel

GHOST MOB II

Stilloan Robinson

MOB TIES I II

By SayNoMore

BODYMORE MURDERLAND I II III

By Delmont Player

FOR THE LOVE OF A BOSS

By C. D. Blue

MOBBED UP

By King Rio

BOOKS BY LDP'S CEO, CA$H

TRUST IN NO MAN

TRUST IN NO MAN 2

TRUST IN NO MAN 3

BONDED BY BLOOD

SHORTY GOT A THUG

THUGS CRY

THUGS CRY 2

THUGS CRY 3

TRUST NO BITCH

TRUST NO BITCH 2

TRUST NO BITCH 3

TIL MY CASKET DROPS

RESTRAINING ORDER

RESTRAINING ORDER 2

IN LOVE WITH A CONVICT

LIFE OF A HOOD STAR

J-Blunt

CPSIA information can be obtained
at www.ICGtesting.com
Printed in the USA
LVHW010126110921
697560LV00018B/1555